M000312413

Just One Tease

A Kingston Family
Dirty Dare Story

NEW YORK TIMES BESTSELLING AUTHOR
Carly Phillips

Copyright © Karen Drogin 2023
Published by CP Publishing
Print Edition

Cover Photo: Wander Aguiar
Cover Design: Maria @steamydesigns
Editing:
Alexis, Sweetheart Author Services
Claire Milto, BB Virtual Assistant for Authors

* * *

Dedication

I haven't written a dedication in a long time, but the Kingston Family has taken two years of my life and my heart and I couldn't have done this alone. As always, thank you to my best friend Janelle Denison aka Erika Wilde. Your support and critique and age, eye color, and name checking make sure these books turn out just right. And a very special thank you to Nicole Andrews Moore for you know why. Zach is for you. I hope you think I did him justice. And to Chasity Jenkins-Patrick for loving Zach as much if not more than Ian and Ethan when I needed to hear it.

Chapter One

H ADLEY STEVENS LOVED her job but this time of year always turned high school kids into fidgety, hormonal savages thanks to being stuck inside a stuffy brick building seven hours a day, five days a week. They were so close to summer freedom, even *she* could relate to their restless spirits.

The sun shone overhead as she walked to her car. Coworkers also strode to their vehicles and Hadley knew without asking they were all grateful it was the second to last Friday of the school year. It helped that the weather was warm, even for mid-June in Braxton, Illinois, giving everyone an extra pep in their step. Hadley had no plans for the weekend beyond reading and relaxing, and if the weather stayed nice, she would sit outside and chill.

The house she lived in with her father, Gregg, and thirteen-year-old sister, Danika, had a small patio in the backyard where Hadley always found peace. No doubt some of this weekend would include shuffling Dani to and from a friend's house, too, something Hadley didn't mind at all.

She approached her car, key fob in hand when a

man strode up beside her, his shadow blocking the sun.

"Hadley Stevens." He said her name in a low voice.

She stiffened and looked up, recognizing him immediately. He was one of the sleazy men who'd been meeting with her father in their home most evenings, hanging out in their family room, and eyeing her just-developing thirteen-year-old sister with lust-filled eyes. Their perversion scared Hadley to no end and she always kept Dani within arm's reach until the men left.

"What do you want?" Hadley slid her finger over the alarm on her key fob.

He grasped her wrist tight enough to bruise. "Don't. Hear me out and nobody has to get hurt." He slid his jacket aside, revealing a holstered gun.

Shaking now, she straightened her shoulders and refused to show more fear. "I'm listening."

"Tell your father if he doesn't do what we asked, we'll take you and your pretty little sister as payment instead." Releasing her wrist, he strode off, mixing in with the male and female teachers in the lot.

Trembling, she could barely unlock her car door and when she finally climbed inside, she jammed her finger against the door-lock button four times before she convinced herself she was safe.

Dani, she thought, her stomach twisting in knots.

She had to get home to her sister. The plan calmed her down enough to drive but the past she'd been told to forget crashed through her mind for the duration of the fifteen-minute trip.

Hadley had just come home from shopping with a friend for last-minute makeup and hair clips for her boyfriend's prom night. She'd been high on life and excited to be his date for the senior prom. He didn't care that she was a junior. She and Zach Dare had been friends for years and a couple for almost eight months. And she planned to give him her virginity on prom night.

Except there'd been no prom. Not for her. And probably not for Zach, either. When Hadley had walked into her house that day eleven years ago, she'd been greeted by her father and the federal agents who'd relocated them that night, changing her name, her identity and altering the course of her life forever. She was sure Zach hated her for abandoning him without a word and did her best not to think about the cute boy she thought she'd loved.

Now, as she approached the home where she'd lived since being uprooted from everything and everyone she knew, that same gut-churning feeling returned. She already knew her father had gotten involved with the wrong people again but this time, she doubted they'd have government protection to keep her and Dani safe.

She pulled into the driveway, relieved to find it empty with no other cars on the street. It didn't mean the men weren't inside the house, but it gave her some hope. She glanced at the small home and though the white paint was chipped in places, she'd done her best to keep the grounds pretty by planting flowers and bulbs that bloomed yearly.

She pulled her car into the garage beside her father's vehicle and tapped the button to close the electric door behind her. Still shaking, she walked inside and paused to listen. It was quiet. She didn't hear men's voices and Dani wasn't blasting loud music. Knowing her sister, she was probably using earbuds and destroying her hearing instead.

Hadley rushed through the hall and into the kitchen to find her father pacing back and forth across the small area. "Dad? What did you do?"

"Hadley!" He spun around, his dark hair, newly threaded with gray, an unruly mess. He made it worse when he ran his hand through the too-long strands. His face was drawn and pale, the lines around his eyes and mouth more pronounced. "I've been waiting for you to get home from work."

She narrowed her gaze. "One of the guys who hangs out here just cornered me by my car at school. He said if he couldn't get what he wanted out of you, he'd take me and Dani as payment instead. What did you get involved in this time?"

"Fuck!" He picked up the cookie jar where she kept Dani's lunch money and threw it against the wall, shattering the ceramic and causing a dent in the plaster.

She flexed her fingers, her palms still damp from her hard grip on the steering wheel on the way home, and her wrist throbbed from where the man had gripped her hard enough to leave bruises.

After placing her heavy tote bag on the kitchen table, she drew a deep breath, preparing herself for whatever disaster was coming.

Then she turned to face her too-silent father.

He rubbed his hands over his bloodshot eyes. "I'm in trouble, baby girl." He only called her that when he was feeling guilty about something. "I need you to take your sister and *go*," he said, his gruff, demanding words shocking her.

She'd known he was in trouble but sending them away? "What are you saying?"

He placed his hands on her shoulders and looked into her eyes. "Get your sister from her room, pack a bag, and leave. Now. Drive far and fast."

Processing his words was impossible. "But…"

He shook his head, his eyes wild. "There's no time. Hurry up."

She nodded, and just like when she was sixteen,

Hadley went on autopilot. She rushed upstairs and knocked on her sister's door. Receiving no answer, she opened it and found Dani with earbuds on while tapping away on her laptop, unaware everything was about to change.

Hadley stepped up to the bed, catching her sister's attention.

Dani yanked out her earbuds and grinned. "Hey, Hads. What's up?"

Hadley managed a smile at the nickname that Dani had used since she was a toddler. It had taken Hadley years not to think of herself as Mia Roberts, her given name, the person she'd been prior to entering WITSEC thanks to her father. Mia, a name Dani had never heard anyone call her since she'd been a baby when they'd been forced to disappear.

"Can you shut that down?" Hadley pointed to the laptop. "We need to talk." And she didn't want any of Dani's friends who might be listening on Facetime overhearing.

Hadley had already decided to be honest with her sister. Dani was a smart, wise-for-her-years kid. She already knew neither of her parents were the most upstanding citizens nor did they associate with decent people. It was Hadley who kept Dani's life as normal as possible.

Dani closed the laptop cover and leaned forward.

"What's wrong?"

"I need you to listen carefully," Hadley said, as she sat down on the mattress.

"You're scaring me." Dani's green eyes were wide with fear and Hadley hated her father for forcing her to put that emotion there.

She had no way to soften the blow, either. "Dad got himself into serious trouble. You and I can't stay here. It's not safe and we need to leave."

"What?" Dani asked, her body jerking, her voice raised.

"I'll explain more in the car but right now, pack as much as you can fit in your rolling suitcase and back-pack and meet me in the kitchen. I need to go do the same thing."

Blinking fast, Dani shook her head. "Wait. For how long because I have so many fun things planned for the last week of school and Amy's having a party next weekend!"

Hadley winced, aware of how her sister felt, knowing she'd miss out on things that seemed so big in her young life. She felt the same when she missed going to prom with Zach. And once Dani realized they were probably going to be gone for a long time, that pain and disappointment would only get worse.

"I'm going to treat you like an adult and be one hundred percent honest. I don't know how long we'll be gone but I will find a way to make it up to you. Right now, just pack, please," she said, hoping just this once, Dani's teenage stubbornness wouldn't kick in.

Dani shook her head. "But mom said she was coming over tonight and I need to be here."

Hadley gritted her teeth, doing her best not to show her aggravation at the mention of Dani's selfish, drug-addict mother.

Hadley's mom died in a car accident when she was thirteen. Instead of staying home with his grieving daughter, her father, Gregg, immediately began hitting the bars at night. It wasn't long before he met, hooked up with, then knocked up Patrice Munson. He moved his pregnant girlfriend into the house where Hadley's mom had lived. Patrice hadn't been interested in helping and Hadley, in between schoolwork and her part-time job, did everyone's share of housework and cooking.

Dani was a year old when the feds moved them as a *family* to a small town in Illinois. And that sent a bored, miserable Patrice into a drug-induced spiral, leaving Hadley to care for Dani just as she had been prior to the move. Ultimately, Patrice lost custody due to her neglect and she only saw Dani because their father allowed it, as long as he or Hadley was home to supervise.

"Hads?" Dani's voice shook Hadley out of her

stupor and put her squarely back in reality. Was it any wonder she'd escaped into her memories, even if it had meant revisiting a shitty past?

"What? I didn't catch what you said." Hadley looked at her sister.

Dani rolled her eyes. "I said, can we please leave *after* I see mom?"

Hadley sighed. "You saw your mom last night." And it was unusual for Patrice to show up two days in a row, let alone all that often. Hadley doubted she'd be returning tonight, disappointing Dani yet again. But she wasn't going to fight with her sister by bringing up the truth about her mom.

"We'll figure out what to do about seeing your mother again but right now, we need to *go*." Hadley walked to the closet and pulled out Dani's suitcase. "Come on, now. Get packing."

Ignoring the half-yell, half-whine from her sister, Hadley rushed to her room, retrieved *her* suitcase, and began to throw things in without thinking.

She dumped her entire underwear drawer into the suitcase, along with some casual clothes, hearing the thump of her diary. A habit she'd kept up from her teenage years. Putting her feelings on paper helped clear her mind.

Nothing could give her that clarity now, as she wondered what she could possibly tell the school district about her sudden leave. She needed an excuse that wouldn't jeopardize her Teacher Loan Forgiveness or get her fired for bailing on them with no warning the last week of the school year. At least she had until Monday morning to think of something.

After she packed, Hadley shut her bedroom door. She walked to her closet and knelt, grateful that ever since their middle-of-the-night move, she'd thought ahead. Beneath three shoe boxes, she pulled out a fourth and opened the top. Inside she had a secret stash. A mix of cash and prepaid Visa and Mastercards she'd saved over the years along with a burner phone. She couldn't say she'd anticipated this moment but something inside her knew she needed to prepare just in case.

She stuffed everything into the inside lining of her everyday tote, hooked the bag on her shoulder, and dragged the suitcase to the kitchen. She passed Dani's room on the way and a quick glance confirmed her sister was packing like she was supposed to.

In the kitchen, her father sat at the table, his head in his hands. The shattered jar still lay on the floor, and it took everything in her not to act on habit by getting the broom and cleaning up his mess.

"Dad?" she asked when he didn't look up.

He rose from his seat and walked over to where she stood. "Take this." He shoved cash in her hand.

"Don't use your credit cards. They're traceable."

As if she hadn't learned that lesson from the female agent who'd accompanied them here when she was sixteen. Hadley glanced back at the destroyed cookie jar and realized he'd gathered up the spare fives and singles she'd stuffed inside.

From the look and feel of the bundle, he'd added more but as she flipped through the pile, her heart sank at the small denomination of the bills. He didn't know she had access to untraceable money, yet this wasn't enough to get by, and her disappointment in him somehow grew.

"This won't even cover a motel. Not if we want to eat. I need more. Is there anything else in the house?" she asked, pushing him because she would eventually need access to more funds.

"I'm here," a sullen Dani said at the same time her father shook his head.

Hadley turned as her sister shuffled into the room. Her backpack hung over one shoulder and she dragged her suitcase behind her. She'd put on a baseball cap and her long hair hung in braids on either side of her head. The front strand she'd dyed pink covered one eye and she glared at them through the other. Looking at her now, no one would realize how beautiful the teen really was.

Their father moved close and pulled Dani into a

long hug. "I'll see you soon. I promise." He met Hadley's gaze over Dani's head, seeming to beg her to make this easier.

He couldn't even handle the goodbye like a man.

"Dani, why don't you meet me in my car? I parked it in the garage. I'll be right out."

The teenager held onto her father for a few seconds longer, enough time for Hadley's anger at their dad to grow. Every time she thought he'd hit his lowest in her estimation, he dug the hole deeper.

Dani released him and looked at Hadley, and she forced a wink at her sister. "It'll be a fun road trip. I promise." Too bad she couldn't cross her fingers behind her back at the lie.

She didn't know what awaited them any more than she knew where they'd go. "Go on and get settled in the car. I'll be right out." Hadley wanted a minute with her father. "You can even pick the music you want to listen to," she said, already cringing at the certainty of loud sound to add to her pounding head.

Once Dani stomped out, Hadley spun around. "I can't believe you did this to her. To us. Again. Don't you ever learn?" She didn't ask him what kind of trouble he was in. The less she knew, the safer she would be.

He hung his head and sighed but didn't answer, which was a good thing. Nothing he said would make any difference.

"Take Dani somewhere safe," he muttered. "And don't tell me where you end up, either."

Of course. Because if he didn't know their whereabouts and those dangerous people came after him, he couldn't reveal their location. Regardless of what they did to him to extract information. She shuddered and nausea threatened.

"I'm sure my calls are being traced," he continued in a monotone but urgent voice. "There's a burner number on a piece of paper stuffed in with the money. Once you're settled, get one for yourself and ring me once so I have your number. That way I can let you know when it's safe to come home."

If it was ever safe, she thought, not saying the words aloud.

He had tears in his eyes but she was in a mixed state of shock, anger, and disbelief, too stunned by the sudden upheaval to feel bad for him. He'd caused this mess.

"I'm sorry." He pulled her into a hug.

One she forced herself to return because a part of her feared this might be the last time she saw her father.

"Go, baby girl."

She stepped back and nodded. "Bye, Dad."

Chapter Two

F OR THE FIRST twenty minutes of the ride Dani was silent, giving Hadley time to think. Too bad she hadn't come up with a destination when Dani finally spoke.

"Are we taking a plane? I've never been on an airplane." She sounded excited which was better than the angry quiet of before.

Hadley shook her head. "We can't. We'd have to show our IDs and I don't want a footprint, digital or otherwise." God, she was repeating the FBI's words verbatim. She supposed there were some things one never forgot.

She slid her gaze to the passenger seat. Dani had scrunched her nose, then nodded. "I get it. I've seen that show called *FBI* on television. What's the plan then?"

Hadley glanced at her gas tank gauge and sighed. She hadn't anticipated a long trip. "Let's hit the next rest stop and load up on snack food. That'll get us by until I'm tired and we can find a motel for the night."

From there, she'd decide where to go next but for now, she was headed east. It was as good a route as any and ironically, she was driving in the direction of New York City and the town where she'd grown up. And the boy, now a man, she'd never forgotten. She wondered if Zach ever thought of her and if so, if he'd forgiven her disappearance. She shook off that thought and focused on the present.

She pulled into a rest stop and filled the car with gas, then parked. She and Dani walked into the store.

Knowing she had to keep her sister happy during this trip, Hadley extended a hand, gesturing to the aisles of chips, candy, soda, and other food. "Load up. And I know you're not a kid but let's both try and use the restroom. It'll save us having to stop again until we're ready to pull over for the night."

"Love the reverse psychology, sis. But I'm still going to roll my eyes and tell you I'd know if I had to pee."

Hadley rolled hers right back. "Try anyway."

A little while later, they were in a long line for the register with a basket full of junk food and drinks, waiting to get their items rung up so she could pay. Dani seemed engrossed in her phone, bopping her head in time to music Hadley could hear above the earbuds.

She tapped her sister on the shoulder and pulled one earbud out of Dani's ear.

"Hey!" The teen objected to the interruption.

"That phone's in airplane mode, right?" Hadley had already told Dani to do that and she'd adjusted her own cell, hoping that would prevent them from being traced or followed. But it didn't hurt to be cautious and make sure Dani had listened.

Dani rolled her eyes. "You told me to when we left home, remember?" She shoved the earbud back into her ear.

She glanced around and her gaze came to rest on one of the few magazines on the endcap rack. The cover photo was a punch to her already painful emotions. A photo of Harrison Dare and his siblings at the Cannes Film Festival for a movie premiere stared back at her. The entire Dare family was in the shot, including Zach, and Hadley's knees went weak at the sight of him for the first time in years.

Since being forced to leave the first time, she hadn't looked him up online because she knew it would be too painful to see him on social media. Not that she'd allowed herself to have a profile of her own. She'd taken every word the feds said to heart. She had no intention of exposing her family, even by mistake. There were people who'd recognize Hadley so she remained as hidden as she could. No one from the past would know Dani, enabling her sister to have all the social media apps along with her friends.

The line ahead of her moved slowly and her gaze

drifted back to Zach's handsome face. No longer a boy, he was all man, and mouth-wateringly handsome. She skimmed the article and discovered that like his siblings, Zach was wealthy and recently famous, thanks to a news article about him that had gone viral. He'd been the person who found the stalker terrorizing Harrison's then-pregnant girlfriend and turning her whereabouts over to the police.

Since Winter Capwell was a reporter, she'd published a story about her ordeal that every news outlet had picked up. A second article followed, this one about Zach and all the people who'd contacted Winter to rave about how he'd helped reunite them with missing family members.

He also owned two bars, one in Manhattan, another in East Hampton. But his side business was finding people who had disappeared, and until the viral news story, he'd done it quietly and under the radar. She blinked as the solution to her own problems came to her. Zach was the perfect person to help her keep Dani safe and though he might not want to see Hadley ever again, she needed him.

And based on what she read about him, Zach Dare would never turn away someone in danger. Especially a young teen and Hadley was more worried about her sister than herself.

"Next!" The cashier called out.

Hadley had been slowly shuffling forward, her focus on the magazine and learning about Zach, and she hadn't realized it was her turn. Dani was still bopping her head to the music, making Hadley grin despite their circumstances.

She unloaded the food from the basket and waited as the woman behind the counter rang up the total and bagged the items.

At the last second, Hadley cleared her throat. "Can you add this please?" She handed over the magazine. If she was lucky, there would be information about Zach inside. Regardless, she now had a photo of him to look at later and prepare herself to see him again.

She paid and they walked back to the car. Dani pulled her earbuds out. "I saw you buy that magazine. Why?"

God, the teenager missed nothing. "There's an article in it I want to read. And I decided where we're headed." She might as well tell her sister the new plan. "We're going to New York City.

"Really? What's in the city?"

"Someone I think can help us," she said as they reached the car and together put the bags into the back seat.

Once they were resettled in the front, Dani buckled her seatbelt and Hadley did the same.

"So, who's this person? Old boyfriend?" Dani

asked.

Hadley choked on her own saliva and began to cough. She wiped her tears and turned to her sister with a narrowed gaze. "What makes you say that?"

"Oops. Mom slipped and told me she met dad in Manhattan. That we used to live in a town nearby but we had to move to Illinois when I was a baby."

Hadley couldn't believe Patrice could be so careless. Then again… yes, she could. "That doesn't explain the boyfriend comment."

Dani shrugged. "Just a guess."

A too lucky one, Hadley thought. Before she could press her sister, Dani shoved the earbuds back into her ears and cranked up the volume.

Happy for the opportunity to put some quiet music on so she could think as she drove, Hadley decided not to yell about the decibel level. Her new plan involved finding a decent motel that took cash and wouldn't insist on seeing her license. No small feat.

She would also have to stop at a public library in Illinois so she could look up the name of Zach's bars. That way nobody could trace her. Once she had the phone number, she'd call and ask to speak to Zach, hoping that would tell her which bar she should go to first.

She planned to hang up before he answered. The first time she spoke to Zach in eleven years had to happen in person and she needed the element of surprise on her side. Maybe then he'd be so happy to see her again, he wouldn't throw her out before she had a chance to explain her sudden disappearance.

ZACH DARE SAT on a barstool, watching in amusement as his niece, Leah, ripped open her birthday gifts with all the exuberance of a seven-year-old. He was surprised her accompanying squeals hadn't yet shattered someone's eardrums.

The good news of the day was she'd had a party for just her friends last weekend and though Zach had stopped by, he hadn't had to deal with all the kids running around and shrieking. Because why speak when yelling was so much fun?

Leah's father and Zach's brother, Nick, hushed her while stuffing the wrapping paper into a big garbage bag, trying his best to keep up with the mess. Nick's wife, Aurora, held their ten-month-old daughter, Ellie, on her lap while writing down who brought each present. The rest of his massive family gathered around, talking and laughing with their significant others, their children and various family friends.

Zach strode over to Remy, his longtime friend and more recently, his business partner. Last year, Remy had retired from his position as a New York City detective and bought into both of Zach's businesses. Together they ran two bars, one in the city and the other in East Hampton, along with a private investigation business.

But there was more to Remy than being a former cop. He kept a low profile but Remington Sterling was one of *The* Sterlings, a family with old-money wealth thanks to a financial equity firm going back generations and real estate holdings all over Manhattan. But like Zach, Remy was wealthy in his own right thanks to a joint venture that had begun back in their college days.

"Hey," Zach said to his friend.

Remy looked up from the iPad he'd been viewing. "Hi. The birthday girl looks like she's having fun. Sounds like it too," he said with a grin.

"Thanks for shutting the restaurant so my family could have a party for Leah," Zach said.

"She calls me Uncle Remy. How could I say no?" Remy asked, chuckling.

Zach grinned. "She does know how to wrap the men of the family around her finger, doesn't she?"

His friend laughed.

"Drink?" Zach walked behind the bar to get himself a soda.

"Diet."

Using the fountain gun, he filled two glasses and slid one across the bar.

He lifted the other for himself and walked back to a stool, taking a seat beside Remy. He faced the alcohol bottles lined up on shelves which were bolted into the wall behind the bar. His family's Dirty Dare brand of spirits took up most of the space and Zach was damned proud. Both of his siblings, their lives and careers, as well as his own.

He took a gulp from his glass, wishing he'd remembered to grab straws.

"So how was your date last night?" Remy asked.

At the question, Zach choked on his soda. "There was no date," he managed to say as he wiped his eyes, which had watered from swallowing wrong.

An attractive bar regular had invited him out to dinner. "I said no, remember? She's not my type," he muttered. But she had been pushy and hadn't liked being turned down.

Remy took a long sip of his drink. "While we're discussing your type, quit hitting on Raven," he said of the woman who'd been a server at the New York City location for a couple of years.

Raven had seen the Help Wanted sign in the window, walked into the bar and handed him two references. One had been from a restaurant where she'd waitressed, the other from a bar where she'd mixed drinks and served. After Zach verified her references, he'd rented her the apartment upstairs and hired her as a server.

She'd provided excellent service to the customers and had become an invaluable employee and friend. She was so good that after Remy had become his partner, and they'd opened a second location last year, they'd promoted Raven to manager. Remy held down the fort in Manhattan and Zach managed the Hamptons.

Not once in the years she'd worked for him had Zach considered sleeping with her. It was Remy who had desired her from the second they'd met.

"Relax. Banter is our thing," Zach reminded him. Whatever Raven's hang-ups about getting involved with Remy, Zach was no threat.

"As long as you remember Raven isn't your type either," Remy muttered.

"I'm not interested in her and she sure as hell isn't attracted to me," he told his friend, realizing his behavior had gotten under his pal's skin.

Remy nodded. "Yeah. It's just… something's bothering her and she's not letting me in."

Zach thought about his New York manager. Something might be off. She'd normally want to oversee a private party, especially one for his or Remy's family, but she'd asked if she could sit this one out. Since Raven pretty much made her own hours, as she did the scheduling for the staff, and was rarely not at work, of course he'd said yes. She said she wasn't feeling well and he'd believed her. But... Remy knew her best.

"Try turning on the charm and if that doesn't work, sit her down and insist you want to know what's going on." Zach attempted to give his friend advice on his love life but other than his siblings' recent relationships and marriages, Zach had little of his own adult experiences to draw from.

One night stands? Yeah, those he could do. Relationships meant exposing too much of himself and he wouldn't go there again.

Remy ran a hand through his too-long hair. Once he'd left the force, he'd gone overboard in growing out his hair and beard. A fuck you to the rules he'd been subjected to as a cop. "I'll think about it," he muttered.

Zach decided a subject change was in order. "Okay so... since you've mentioned it twice, just what *is* my type?" He was curious what his friend thought considering Remy had never seen Zach with a woman more than once or twice.

Remy smirked at the question. "If I had to describe her, I would say she's understated but beautiful, has ample curves but isn't overly voluptuous." He drummed his fingers on the counter as he continued to think.

Meanwhile, Zach couldn't believe Remy had nailed Zach's ideal woman, at least the way she looked. The one perfect female who'd had his heart back when he'd believed settling down was in his future. God, he'd been young. And stupid.

The sound of Remy slurping the end of his drink pulled Zach out of his musings.

"In other words," Remy said, "She's the opposite of anyone I've ever seen you with. Someone like... *her*." He pointed towards the bar's entrance before turning back to Zach–who spun to face the door.

He took one look at the woman standing with her hand on a teenager's shoulder and felt the blood drain from his face. He blinked, certain he was mistaken. He must be imagining her because Remy had been spot-on in his description and Zach had been trying not to remember too much about her.

Remy stood up beside him. "What's wrong? You look like you've seen a ghost."

He slammed a hand down and curled a spare napkin into a wrinkled ball. "That's because I fucking have."

Chapter Three

Z ACH NEVER EXPECTED the girl he'd once loved to walk into his bar. The last time he'd seen Mia Stevens, he'd dropped her off after school and the next time he planned to see her was when he picked her up for prom the next night. Except when he'd shown up in a rented limousine, dressed in his tuxedo, and holding a wrist corsage, no one answered the door.

Odd, considering Mia had a baby sister and her stepmother was usually home. The neighbors had seen him knocking on the door and come out to tell him the house had been unusually quiet all day.

It turned out, Mia and her family were gone for good. She'd ghosted him not just for prom, which was humiliating enough, but for all the things they'd planned for the future. Zach had done his best to search for her online and when he came up empty, he honed his computer and hacking skills to dig even deeper. Nothing had ever turned up.

Zach drew a deep breath and pushed off the chair, preparing himself to confront her for the first time.

"Zach," Remy said, placing a hand on his shoulder.

"I don't know who she is or what's going on but you look pissed. Maybe I should handle this—"

He shook his head. "I've got it."

Remy released his grip but stayed close behind as Zach strode to the entrance.

Mia hadn't taken a step into the bar, obviously waiting for his reaction. She looked good. Older, obviously, but just as gorgeous, despite being tired, as evidenced by the dark circles beneath her blue eyes. She was still his fresh-faced girl. Her freckles were more pronounced, her brown hair was longer, and though she wore little makeup, her pouty lips still begged to be kissed.

Fuck. She wasn't his, hadn't been in years, and wouldn't be again.

He scrubbed a hand over his face. "It's been a long time, Mia."

She jerked and shook her head. "It's Hadley, now." Her voice had the same, husky quality he remembered.

He narrowed his gaze at the name change.

"And this is my little sister, Danika."

It had been Danielle, he thought, remembering her baby sister. Danika. Another name change.

"It's Dani." The teenager with a pink streak in the front of her hair crossed her arms over her chest and stared at him. From her lack of shyness to the bold hair choice, she was both more outgoing and more of a rebel than her sister had been.

"Hey, Dani," he said.

She looked from Zach to her sister, her nose scrunched as she watched them.

"Zach, I know this must be a shock but can we talk?" Mia—Hadley, he mentally corrected himself, asked.

As much as he wanted to hug her tight, feel her body against his and ask where she'd been all these years, he wouldn't give her the satisfaction of showing any emotion.

Whatever answers she held, she'd opted to keep to herself for the last decade. *He* hadn't been hard to find and she could have come to see him long before now.

Her leaving had been a shock followed by embarrassment when he'd had to face the kids in his class, but her ongoing silence had devastated him. He wouldn't fall at her feet in gratitude she'd shown up now.

"Sorry, but we're closed for a private party." He gestured with a tip of his head toward where his family gathered in the main dining area. "You can show yourselves out."

Her eyes opened wide, flashing with hurt before she banked the emotion.

Forcing himself not to react or show he cared, he turned, intending to walk away, aware of Remy's disapproving stare. His friend didn't have a clue who Mia–Hadley–whatever she called herself had been to him. Although since he'd confided in Remy one drunken night, his friend might be figuring things out.

"*This* is the guy you said would help us?" he heard Dani ask in a sarcastic voice. He paused mid-step. "Good job, sis."

"Be quiet," Hadley hissed. "You have no idea what happened between us."

"So, he's not the boyfriend you had and the prom date you had to ditch when dad screwed–"

Dani's voice cut off.

"We'll discuss how you know about *that* later," Hadley warned the teenager.

He looked over his shoulder to see her hand covering her sister's mouth and he bit the inside of his cheek in an attempt not to laugh. The kid had spunk and though Hadley was probably used to dealing with her, the flush in her cheeks revealed Dani had embarrassed her.

Zach blew out a breath and forced himself to pivot back to them. Dani had had him at the word *help*. Saving women was his weakness, for reasons that began with his mother and the way her life came to a tragic end.

But he couldn't bring himself to make this easy on Hadley. "Fine. Let's talk." His tone was deliberately cool.

She glanced at her sister. "Go sit at a table. I want to talk to Zach in private. I'll come back for you in a few minutes."

Zach glanced at Remy. "Can you get Dani a menu and let her order whatever she wants?" The cook had come in today for Leah's party and would be happy to whip up whatever the teenager wanted.

Remy nodded. "Come on, kid. We've got milkshakes, burgers and anything else you want to eat."

"Sweet. I'm starving. We've been eating crap since we left—"

Hadley managed an impressive eye roll at the same time she slapped a hand over her sister's mouth. Again. "Go eat and do not talk."

Remy chuckled and Dani rushed for a table near the kitchen.

Hadley shook her head and grinned as she watched her sister go. "That kid is a handful," she muttered but Zach saw the love in her eyes and it caused an unwilling tug on his heart.

"Let's go to my office where we won't be interrupted." He extended his arm in the right direction, grateful his family was occupied with the party girl and her presents in another area of the bar.

Hadley-it was going to take time to get used to calling her by that name—nodded and walked ahead of him to the hallway where his office was located.

He'd had years for his anger and hurt to build but he couldn't deny his curiosity about her was still strong. And as she walked to his office, her ass swaying in tight black jeans, he was forced to acknowledge that relief wasn't the only thing he felt upon seeing her again.

NERVES FLUTTERED IN Hadley's stomach as she walked through the bar to Zach's office. The décor she passed appeared old-looking by design with dark distressed wood tables and chairs, but the graffiti and hand-painted art on the walls brought some current style into the mix.

Walking into Zach's office, she looked around, seeing if she could glean any information about the man he'd grown to be. The area was neat with a plain wood-styled desk that could be found in any office supply store and an executive-style leather chair. On the white walls hung family pictures but none were Zach's relatives, at least none she remembered meeting in the past. But everyone had grown up and changed, including her.

"Have a seat." He gestured to one of two open-arm guest chairs across from the desk.

She lowered herself into a chair. "Who are all those people in the pictures?"

"Happy clients," he said, not elaborating further. "And we're not here to talk about me. What did Dani mean by you need help?" He perched himself on the edge of his desk, leaning away from her. The emotional walls he'd erected couldn't be higher, not that she blamed him.

She'd gone over what to say to him during their many hours on the road, but now that she was here, all her ideas disappeared. She took a moment to gather her thoughts, but her gaze cataloged the changes in him instead.

He wore a solid black T-shirt and his muscles were evident below the short sleeves. His chest was broad, his body obviously tight and built. He was all facial scruff and his attitude screamed alpha bad-boy, which begged the question. Where had her lean computer geek gone?

"I'm waiting." His gruff voice startled her and she jumped.

Right. He wanted her story, not for her to sit and ogle him. "Maybe I should start with why I left all those years ago," she said, blurting out the first thing that came to mind.

He folded his arms across his chest and somehow

those biceps bulged even more. "How about you start with why you're here now, instead? No need to revisit the past."

She closed her eyes and sighed. Perhaps she'd misjudged how difficult he'd be. "Fine. My father is in trouble with some very bad people. I know that sounds like a line from a cheesy movie but it's true. One of them approached me by my car after work and said to tell my father if he didn't cooperate, they'd take me and Dani instead. As payment."

Zach's gorgeous indigo eyes narrowed. "Go on."

She swallowed hard. "After he threatened me, the guy left. I got into my car and drove home." She curled her fingers around her handbag until her nails dug into her palms. "As soon as I walked into the house, my father told me to pack up, take Dani, and run."

She met Zach's gaze, hoping to see some form of understanding only to find a stoic mask of indifference. He'd never been cold to her before and despite expecting it, his attitude hurt.

"How did you find me?" he asked. "Actually, scratch that since I already know the answer. *I* wasn't the one who left. A simple Google search would have shown you my location."

God, she'd hurt him and the knowledge twisted inside her.

"Why come to *me* for help?"

Her heart pounded painfully in her chest. If she didn't convince him to help her, she didn't know where she'd go or what to do.

She ran a hand through her hair with a shaking hand. "I read the article your sister-in-law wrote about her ordeal last year. How you were responsible for finding the former senator's wife after she'd attempted to run over Winter with her car. I also read the follow-up about all the families who were indebted to you for what you'd done for them."

She glanced at the photos on the walls again and the pieces fell into place. "They all sent you these." Looking at the good he'd done, warmth filled her up inside, and she was awed by his second occupation. Finding missing people wouldn't always have a happy ending and he did it anyway. "I always knew you'd do great things."

"Don't." He bit out the harsh word and she flinched. At least she was getting some emotion out of him, even if it was anger.

He pushed himself off the desk and paced around the room in silence.

She wondered if he was trying to find a way to say no or if he was attempting to come up with a plan. She hoped it was the latter.

"You need protection," he said at last. "A place to

stay where your sister is safe and so are you." It wasn't a question.

She blew out a long breath and nodded. "Yes. My father asked me to call on my burner phone so he'd have my untraceable number. He'll let us know when it's safe to return."

Closing her eyes, she sighed. "*If* it's ever safe. But right now, I can't worry about that. I need a short-term solution while I figure out what to do next. I can't stay in a hotel because I can't show my license or use my credit cards and they always want to have one on file. I do have some prepaid ones but I'd rather save them for food and emergencies."

Zach stopped pacing and leveled his gaze on hers, as if trying to figure her out.

"You know an awful lot about disappearing without a trace," he muttered, affirming her thought.

She rose to her feet, prepared for an argument but before she could remind him he hadn't *wanted* an explanation, he spoke.

"How did you get here?"

"I drove my car. It's parked behind the bar."

"Is it a newer model?" he asked.

She shook her head. "No." She couldn't control the laugh at the thought of her old vehicle. "Not even close."

Zach had come from a wealthy family but Hadley

was the girl from the wrong side of the tracks. It had been a miracle his parents never gave him a hard time for dating her. Not that she knew of, anyway and they'd always been kind.

"Good." He nodded in approval. "And you never bought a GPS tracking device?"

This time her laugh was even louder. "No, if someone was stupid enough to steal that car, I'd say good riddance and pray I never saw it again."

His gaze caught hers and the first signs of a smirk lifted his lips as they shared an amused smile. She felt a small sense of victory until he caught himself and smoothed out his expression.

"Let's go."

"Where?" she asked as he turned and started for the door without answering.

She rolled her eyes, sick of his attitude.

Before Zach could exit, a knock sounded and the door opened.

The man who stood behind Zach earlier stepped inside. "Just making sure you're both in one piece," he said with a grin she'd have found sexy if she wasn't still so drawn to Zach and the bad boy he'd obviously become. "I'm Remy Sterling. Zach's partner," he said before Zach could perform any introductions. Assuming he even wanted her to meet his friends.

"Hadley Stevens," she said softly. It was up to

Zach to explain who she was–rather, had been to him.

"We were just coming out to discuss some things. Is my family still here?" Zach asked.

Remy's lips lifted in a huge grin. "They sure are and asking where you disappeared to. Dani was only too happy to fill them in." He glanced at her and winked.

"Eyes on me, asshole," Zach muttered.

Her lips parted in surprise.

"Not so fun when the shoe's on the other foot, is it?" Remy asked. "Try and remember that next time you're flirting with Raven."

Hadley had no idea what the byplay between them was about but she wondered. Who was Raven? And what was that sudden jealous knot in her stomach?

"I'll let them all know you're coming out." As Remy turned and walked out, his words finally registered.

"Your *family* is here?" He'd said the restaurant was closed for a private party but she hadn't thought about who it was for.

"It's my niece's birthday. Nick and his wife are having Leah's party here." Zach grimaced. No doubt at the thought of dealing with all the Dares.

How would she face them again? No doubt they were as angry at her for disappearing as their brother was.

Could things get any more difficult? Hadley stifled the

urge to cry in frustration.

"Come on. Might as well get this over with." Zach opened the door and walked into the hall, leaving her to follow him.

Chapter Four

ZACH STRODE OUT of his office, walked down the hall and into the restaurant to find the birthday party had moved from the more open restaurant area to the smaller side by the bar where there were limited tables and stools.

He glanced back at Hadley, who'd grown pale at the sight of them all. Did it make him a bad person that he enjoyed her discomfort? He really needed to get past his old anger because his gut told him the disappearance and move had been outside her control, and had everything to do with her father.

"Hads!" Dani's yell caught his attention.

Hadley strode past him and rushed over to the table where her sister sat beside Layla, Zach's fifteen-year-old half-sister.

Zach rushed to catch up with her, ignoring his sister Jade's whispered question, asking how he was holding up. Right now, he had no idea. Hopefully he'd figure out the answer before he had to reach out and reassure her he was fine.

"Hello, Hadley," his stepmother, Serenity said, a soft smile on her face.

Serenity was more Zach's mom than his birth mother had been. She had moved in as the nanny before he was born and raised all four boys and Jade, doing a mother's job when their own mom couldn't. Serenity hadn't become involved with his father, Michael, until after Audrey's death and they'd had triplets six years later. Five years after that came Layla, the oops baby.

With his mother's mental health issues and her death by suicide, Serenity was the only mom he knew. Which meant she'd known Mia... Hadley, dammit, as well.

"Hi, Mrs. Dare," Hadley said, as if she were still the teenager she used to be.

Serenity laughed. "Please, call me Serenity."

"Thanks for looking out for Dani." Hadley's gaze swept the table and her eyes opened wide. "What did you do? Order everything on the menu?" she asked, obviously horrified by the amount of food on the table.

"He said I could order whatever I wanted," she said, her gaze zeroing in on Zach.

A half-eaten hamburger, French fries, what looked like a cola in a glass, the mac and cheese Zach's bar was known for, and a huge ice cream sundae were in front of Dani right now.

He liked this kid and he couldn't help but laugh. "I

suppose I did."

"Hads, this is Layla. She's older than me but we have a lot in common." Dani pointed to his half-sister. "She told me not to miss out on the mac and cheese, so of course I had to try it."

"Of course, you did. Hi, Layla. Nice to meet you," Hadley said.

"Girls, I need to talk to Michael and Serenity." Zach tipped his head, indicating Layla should take Dani and give them a few minutes.

In typical teen fashion, she rolled her eyes but pushed back her chair. "C'mon, Dani. Take your sundae and we'll go sit somewhere so the *grownups* can talk."

Dani glanced at her sister, as if for permission.

"Go. I'll let you know when we have a plan." Hadley gave her sister the same head tip Zach had used and the kids pushed out of their seats.

Once they were gone, Zach pulled out a chair for Hadley.

She lowered herself down and he dragged another chair over for himself, dropping into it.

He met his parents' curious stares. "Obviously you know some of the details because you called her Hadley not Mia."

"Dani told us they were *on the run*," Michael said, using air quotes with his fingers.

Hadley sighed. "Dani's got a way with words," she muttered. "That's one way of putting it. My father landed himself in trouble and sent us away. I'd read the article on Zach helping his sister-in-law last year and thought maybe he'd be able to... help us, too. Despite me... disappearing back in high school." She looked down, obviously unable to meet anyone's gaze, as she clasped her hands together on the table and turned silent.

The ball was in his court. Though he'd stiffened at the reminder, this wasn't news to anyone at the table. And he'd promised himself to try and get over the past.

After all, she had prepaid cards on hand. Why would she have kept them ready if she hadn't sensed a need?

"My son will always do what's right. So will we. So how can we help?" Michael asked.

Zach ran a hand through his hair and leaned forward, one arm on the table. "I can't say I'm happy with the solution I've come up with but it's all I've got and I need your help." He looked to his father who'd always been there for him.

Michael gave him a slight nod. "What do you want us to do?"

"Since Dani seems to have hit it off with Layla despite the age difference, that should make my idea an easier sell."

Serenity laughed. "Dani certainly is wise and mature for her age."

"What are you talking about?" Hadley asked.

Zach drew a deep breath, prepared for an argument. "Dani should go home with my parents."

"But—"

He held up a hand, cutting her off. "Let me explain. My parents are staying in the Hamptons for the summer and I'm there almost full time now to run the new bar. Remy's in charge here. We're all just here for the birthday party. In East Hampton, the house is gated and you need a code for entry. *No one* can get through the perimeter of the home."

"No." Hadley shook her head. "I'm not going to be separated from my sister right now." She folded her arms across her chest, her tone firm and unwavering.

"Even if her staying with them keeps her safe from anyone who might find *you*?"

She paled and he felt like a shit for his phrasing.

"Zachary." Serenity chided, obviously agreeing.

He leaned forward. "I'm just saying, it's a way to keep everyone safe. Plus, if Dani's with Layla she'll be kept busy and she won't have time to think about everything that's going on. She'll be doing makeup and shopping and all the shit my sister likes to do. Meanwhile, Hadley can get other issues sorted. And I'll explain more about what that means, later."

New cell phones, fixed laptops, making them untraceable.

Hadley looked to Serenity and Michael. "I appreciate the offer and I don't mean to sound ungrateful. Are you *sure* you don't mind? I'd hate to make trouble for either of you."

At least she was considering the idea, Zach thought.

Reaching across the table, Serenity touched Hadley's arm. "Honey, whatever reason you disappeared, given your age at the time, I'm sure you had no choice." She tucked a strand of her dark, shoulder-length hair behind her ear. "You were like family then and you still are. We're happy to take Dani with us."

Leave it to his mom to be so pragmatic and forgiving. He wished he could do the same but he wasn't ready. He knew he'd have to get there but he needed to process the shock of Hadley's return, first.

"Then yes. Thank you," Hadley said. She turned to Zach. "So according to this plan of yours, who's taking me in?"

"I'd be happy to." Remy walked up behind him, bracing his hands on the back of the chair.

Zach refrained from telling his friend to fuck off in front of his parents. "You're staying with me."

Remy chuckled.

Hadley's eyes opened wide. "I'm not so sure that's a good idea."

Neither was he but he wouldn't compromise on the issue. "You came to me for help and this is what I think is best."

He didn't want to get into more in front of his family—his parents at the table, his siblings nearby—all of whom were watching with undisguised interest.

"Fine. But I need to explain things to Dani." Once again, she looked at his parents, her expression turning soft and sweet. "I cannot thank you enough. If you need me for anything…"

"Call me," Zach interrupted. "I'm getting them new, untraceable phones."

"I have them in airplane mode," she said. "I'm sure what we have is fine."

Shit. "Airplane mode doesn't protect you from being traced. It turns off Wi-fi and cellular but not GPS."

Her lips parted wide in surprise.

He sighed. "I get why you would think that makes you safe. It's a normal lay-person assumption. Give me your phones now. This way if anyone traced you here, we don't want to lead them to your next destination. Like I said, I'll get you both new ones tomorrow."

Once again, Hadley stiffened and he knew he was in for an argument about cost later.

She slid out of her chair and strode over to where

the teenagers sat.

Remy slid into her vacated chair, and Zach felt, rather than saw, some of his siblings close in around him.

"Okay, I'm not doing this," he said to them. "My gut tells me Hadley will be around for a while so you can all get your answers in time. Right now Dani's staying with Mom and Dad, and Hadley will be with me. They need help and I'm providing it. End of discussion." He pushed his chair out and stood.

"Watch my foot," Nick muttered.

Zach hadn't realized Nick was behind him.

"I just wanted to say goodbye and thanks for hosting the party. Ellie's cranky and Leah wants to go home and play with her toys."

Zach rose and said goodbye to his siblings who were all doing the same with each other.

"Leah, come give me a hug, birthday girl!" he called out to his niece.

She ran over and wrapped her skinny arms around his neck. "Will you come over and play with my karaoke machine with me?" she asked, practically vibrating with excitement.

"I will," he said, chuckling at the gift he'd bought her. He'd had to Google what to buy a seven-year-old girl but if her screams had been anything to go by when she'd peeled off the wrapping paper, he'd hit gold.

"I'll get you back for that gift," Aurora, Nick's wife said, giving Zach a kiss on the cheek, Ellie in her arms.

"Bye, chunky monkey," he said to the baby with big cheeks and a bigger smile.

Once the place had emptied out, leaving Remy to oversee the employees cleaning up, Zach turned to his parents. "We'll go to the back parking lot together. I want to move Hadley's car into my designated parking spot so nobody will bother it. Dani can grab her bag and you guys can head out. Call or text me when you're home and settled."

"I will." His father slapped him on the back. Michael Dare, with his salt-and-pepper hair and the Dare indigo eyes, glanced at Zach like he wanted to say something.

When he merely shook his head, Zach breathed out a sigh of relief. He needed time before he spoke about Hadley's return with anyone.

Hadley handed him the keys to her car and he moved the vehicle into his private, empty spot. He'd text and ask Remy to let Raven and the staff know not to assume it was an illegally parked car and call for a tow.

After he parked the car, he climbed out and stepped over to where his parents stood with Layla, Hadley and Dani.

Hadley turned to her sister, a worried look on her face and a sheen of tears in her eyes. "Be good and be smart. And don't give the Dares a hard time. They're doing us a favor, okay?"

"Yes, *mom*," Dani said, but her easy grin told Zach she respected her sister's words. "Don't worry. I'll behave."

"Hey, kid? I hate to do this but I want to get you a new cell phone that I'm sure is safe. Think you can give up yours for the night? I'll pick up a new one tomorrow and bring it over. Laptop too. I want to install some safety protocols." Like a VPN that would keep her internet private.

He saw the indecision on Dani's face. A teenager forced to disconnect from social media wasn't an easy ask. Though it was nonnegotiable, he'd rather she give up the items on her own so she didn't hate him for taking them. Why he cared what she thought of him, he hadn't a clue.

"Can I get a brand new iPhone, then? The one with the big screen?" the little con artist asked.

He'd seen her phone earlier. The screen was cracked, and the model was old. "Sure."

"No!" Once again, Hadley's eyes were wide, her sensual lips parted in shock at her sister's antics. "Don't be a brat. Hand it all over and you'll get the cheapest model and be happy with it."

With a pout that turned to a smile after Zach privately winked at her, Dani walked to the back of his parents' SUV and pulled out her phone and laptop. "Here you go." She handed the electronics to him and he tucked the laptop under his arm.

"Thanks, kid."

Hadley sighed. "I'll pay you back when I can. I promise."

Another argument she'd lose, he thought. "Okay everyone, we're out."

Another round of goodbyes followed and finally, Hadley climbed into Zach's large, black SUV. Seatbelts clicked, he started the engine, put the vehicle in drive and pulled out of the parking lot behind the bar.

As if she understood his need for quiet or maybe she needed time to think too, Hadley sat in silence, not even asking where he lived. Her quiet demeanor left him the opportunity to sort through his own feelings. Seeing her again had been a shock. Having her in his life, in his home, no matter how temporary, wouldn't be easy.

Not for the first time since coming up with the idea of separating the sisters, he questioned his judgment. He could have put Hadley up in a hotel with his credit card and she'd probably have been safe. But that was an assumption. He couldn't be certain about anything. Keeping Hadley in his Hamptons home was the safest bet.

But there was more to his decision. A part of him *wanted* Hadley by his side. For over ten years, he hadn't a clue where she'd been. Despite his anger, he didn't want her out of his sight now that she'd returned. Not that he'd admit as much to her. He'd barely come to terms with that truth himself.

When it came to Hadley Stevens, he was a tightly wound ball of conflict, and he didn't see those feelings shifting any time soon.

Chapter Five

HADLEY HADN'T GIVEN a thought to where she'd stay once she found Zach. All she'd cared about was taking Dani somewhere safe. Even if she'd let her mind go there, moving into Zach's house would never have crossed her mind.

Yet here she was.

Even she had to admit, Dani was well-protected with Zach's parents. And her sister had been thrilled to stay with Layla, aware she would have more fun at the Dares than she would with her sister.

Now, after a long, quiet car ride from the city to East Hampton, Zach pulled into a driveway that led to a gorgeous home on the water. A gate surrounded the property with immaculately groomed shrubbery and flowers out front.

Despite knowing his family was wealthy, she hadn't been prepared for the size and luxuriousness that greeted her. "Your family hotel business must be doing well," she murmured.

He raised an eyebrow at her comment. "Believe it or not, I don't touch my family money." He opened his window and punched a code into a standing keypad, and the gate at the beginning of the driveaway slowly opened.

"The bars and PI business are this lucrative?" She wasn't ashamed to ask the question nor was she being snarky. Zach's family status was well known and she was curious about him.

He drove up the driveaway, stopped the car and tapped the garage remote. The car idled as they waited for the electric door to open.

"Actually, I made my money in computer software." He didn't elaborate and she bit back a sigh at his reluctance to open up.

She'd known he was great with numbers and computers. They'd met when he'd been assigned to tutor her in math class but for this kind of money, he'd obviously advanced his skills in the years since.

He pulled the SUV into the garage parking space, cut the engine and opened his door. She hopped out her side. In silence, he pulled her bag from the back and walked to the door. Although he obviously had no intention of letting her into his life, thoughts, or history, his house was another story.

After disabling the alarm, he led her inside.

Now that they were alone, she wanted to talk to him and explain about her past, hoping the story would dull the edges of his lingering resentment.

They entered the living room and the floor to ceiling windows with a view of the ocean stunned her with its beauty.

She walked closer to the glass for a better view when the sound of Zach's phone ringing jarred her and she turned.

He pulled the cell from his pocket and glanced at the screen before answering. "Hey, Maddox. Problem?" He listened, a scowl forming on his handsome face the longer the person on the other end spoke. "Yeah. I'm coming. See you soon."

Her stomach dropped at the news he was leaving.

He disconnected the call and shoved the phone back into his jeans. "There's a problem at my bar in town."

"Is that the one you run?"

He nodded. "Remy likes to stay in Manhattan and keep an eye on Raven. Not that she needs watching."

His low chuckle told her there was something more between Raven and his partner than just business. Or Remy wanted there to be. It was a vibe she'd caught earlier in Zach's office.

"If you walk down the hall that way, there are a couple of guest bedrooms. Pick one and make yourself at home." He glanced at her bag he'd dropped at his feet. "Actually, I'll put this in one of the bedrooms for you."

She shook her head. "I've got it. You go. You're

needed at the bar." Though she wanted to argue that she needed him here, she couldn't do it. His business was more important than her wanting to set things right between them.

He nodded. "I'll write my cell phone down on the way out and leave it by the landline in the kitchen. I keep one for emergencies. If you need anything, call. But I promise, you're safe here. I'll set the alarm before I go."

"Okay," she murmured, relieved there was a working phone in the house. Just in case, she wouldn't use hers until she'd bought a new one tomorrow. And the burner was only for emergencies to reach her father, something she'd do before turning in tonight.

Zach shoved a hand into his pocket and pulled out his keys, spinning the ring around his finger. "The fridge is full and the freezer has precooked meals you can microwave. Harrison found himself a housekeeper. Mrs. Baker cooks like a dream and I sweet-talked her into working for me, too." His sexy lips lifted in a grin.

She'd just bet he had. "Thanks. I'll be fine."

He inclined his head, holding her gaze for long seconds, before turning and walking out, leaving her alone.

ZACH COULDN'T DENY his relief at being called back to the bar. No matter the issue, and missing liquor inventory *was* a problem, he'd rather deal with that than be alone with Hadley. Which was ironic. He'd spent years thinking of her and wondering what had happened to her. Now she was here and the main emotion riding him was anger over the fact that she'd waited so long to come find him.

Pushing those thoughts aside, he parked his SUV in a spot behind the bar and walked in through the back entrance. He'd expected to find Maddox waiting for him. He was. With Remy by his side.

"What are you doing here?" he asked his partner, who'd been in Manhattan a few hours ago.

Remy picked up a rag and ran it over the top of the bar. "Do you think I would leave my closest friend to go through a shock like you've had alone?"

Zach strode to the bar. "I appreciate it." And he'd do the same for Remy so he understood.

"Let's deal with the inventory issues and then I want to hear how it's going with… Hadley. That *is* her name now, right?" Remy asked.

Zach nodded. "Apparently."

Maddox stepped closer. "There are bottles missing from the storage room, boss. They were there when the deliveries arrived. I counted and sorted them myself."

Zach's gut told him to trust Maddox. The man didn't need to steal from the bar. He was a burned out Wall Street investment manager who'd done well for himself and moved to the Hamptons to get away from the drain of his old life and the people in it.

"Okay, do a full inventory of what we have in stock. I know we're short on staff so look into hiring someone to free you up from behind the bar. I'll put a lock on the door of supply room and we'll figure shit out."

Maddox inclined his head. "You got it." He walked away, leaving Zach with Remy.

His friend didn't wait to grill him. "So, what did you find out about Hadley? Why the name change? Where has she been? Why did she disappear?" He tossed the rag into a bin behind him and turned back, obviously waiting for an answer.

Lowering himself into a chair, Zach admitted, "I haven't a clue. I didn't ask."

Remy narrowed his gaze. "You had hours in the car to talk. Why the hell not?"

With a groan, Zach gripped the back of his neck with one hand, the tension knotting his muscles unbearable. "Because once I know, I'll have to forgive her and I'm not ready."

Remy nodded in understanding. "I get it."

"I'm not sure how to explain it but she's the sole

58

reason my life took the turn that it did." In his obsessive need to find her, he'd taken his computer skills from legit to the darker world of hacking.

With Remy's help while in college, they'd come this close to breaking into a government database. Whether it had the information he'd needed, Zach didn't know. Because the feds showed up on his doorstep before he'd hit paydirt.

"So we were arrested for hacking. Big fucking deal. It's not like we went to jail. Not only did we end up doing government work, we also made the contacts to sell our anti-hacking software for a hefty fortune. Can't say your life sucks," he said, taking a long sip. "Neither does mine."

Remy pulled out the bottle of bourbon they reserved for nights like this one. He reached for two old fashioned glasses and treated them each to a pour.

Zach lifted his glass and Remy did the same. "No, life is pretty damned good now. But if Hadley tells me about her past, at some point, I'll need to do the same." And that admission would reveal how desperate he'd been to find her.

Once they stopped hacking, he stopped searching. He hadn't made peace with her disappearance and as time went on, knowing she could have reached out to him at any time had helped turn his obsession to find her into the anger he held onto now.

Once he spoke the truth to Hadley, he'd have to let that anger go. And the feelings he'd pushed down deep would resurface. Feelings she no longer deserved.

Needing both the fortification and the numbness sure to follow, he finished off his drink.

"So I take it I'm going to have to run that background check on her after all," Remy said. "Now that I have her new name."

Zach shrugged. "Do what you need to do," he said, ignoring the guilt that statement brought.

Remy narrowed his gaze. "Or you could get the truth directly from her."

"Even if I let her explain, I'd still want to verify and make sure she told me everything."

Really? A voice in his head asked. Was he really that suspicious of Hadley? The self-protective part of him said yes, he didn't know the woman who'd walked into his bar but the younger, less jaded side of him, told him he could trust her.

Which voice in his head did he believe?

Remy placed his glass on the table and rested one elbow on the bar. "She's here of her own free will and scared out of her mind. I don't think she's going to be holding shit back from you now." Picking up the bottle, he refilled both glasses. "I think she'll be pissed if we dig into her past when she's already told you she's willing to talk. Why don't you listen and decide afterwards if you think she's revealed it all? You have good instincts. Trust them."

Remy had a point. He needed to hear her out.

A decade ago, she'd upended his life when she disappeared. Now she'd done the same thing by reappearing out of the blue.

Remy went home to the house he had in East Hampton to get some sleep. He wanted to wake up early to drive back to the city. And Zach moved to a booth, settling in for the duration because he had no intention of going home until long after his houseguest was asleep.

He hadn't had another drink since the two pours with Remy and he sat alone, watching the thickening crowd of people fill the establishment. He was happy they'd decided to open a second Back Door Bar in the Hamptons. It had been a solid business decision when Remy asked if he could buy in.

Soon his mind turned to Hadley puttering around his huge house, by herself. After two days of driving cross country to escape men who'd threatened her.

And he'd left her alone.

Fuck.

He pushed himself out of the booth and stopped by the office where Maddox sat at a desk, looking over what appeared to be inventory sheets.

"I'm out," he told the other man. "We'll get to the

bottom of things. I'm sure it's an accounting error. Or an employee who thinks we won't miss a couple of bottles." If that were the case, Zach had every intention of making sure the person was fired. He wouldn't put up with someone stealing from him.

"Thanks. I'll figure this out. It happened on my watch and that pisses me off," Maddox muttered.

Zach inclined his head, respecting the man's ethics. "See you tomorrow."

"Night."

Zach drove home from the bar and parked his car inside the garage. He let himself into the house and silence surrounded him. She was asleep, he thought, grateful for the reprieve. He strode through the hallway and walked into the large living area, taking in the muted lights he normally shut off before turning in for the night. Hadley must have left them on so she wouldn't feel lost in the new-to-her house.

A low, sexy murmur reached his ears. He followed the sound into the living room, glancing at the couch where Hadley had fallen asleep. She lay with her head on a throw pillow, her soft brown hair covering her cheek. Damn, she was just as beautiful now. More so, with the curves and fullness of a woman and not that of a teenage girl.

He knew he could fall for her again, so easily.

He shook off the thought, took a step toward his

bedroom and stopped. He couldn't leave her sleeping like this. She'd wake up with a stiff neck.

He strode to the sofa, bent and scooped her into his arms. As he lifted and adjusted her body against him, her lashes fluttered open.

"Zach?" she murmured.

"Shh. I'm just taking you to bed. You fell asleep in the living room."

"I waited up for you," she said in a husky, sleep-filled voice as she wrapped one arm around his neck. "Want to talk."

He breathed in deep, taking in her warm, floral scent and even if it was his imagination, her fragrance smelled familiar. His cock hardened at that, not to mention the feel of her in his arms.

"In the morning," he promised. It was time.

He started for the bedrooms, walking through the house and toeing open her door. He placed her on the bed, not realizing her arm remained hooked around his neck and he found them face to face. Nose to nose. Her lips a breath away. His heart beat rapidly in his chest and he couldn't not give in.

Closing the distance, he brushed her lips with his before pulling out of her hold. "Night, Hads. Get some sleep."

She rolled over and was out cold before he left the room, not that he blamed her. She'd had a traumatic day and there was more to come. Starting tomorrow.

Chapter Six

HADLEY STOOD IN Zach's kitchen. The large window by the sink overlooked the pale sand leading to the back of the house and the beach beyond. The view was gorgeous, as was the decor, and as always with the Dares, way out of her league and beyond her comprehension. She only had to look at her used car and the house she lived in back home to know that. But Zach, his siblings and parents, never made her feel less than, something that in her eyes, made this family unique.

She picked up her coffee cup and blew on the brew before taking a sip. "Mmm." She needed the caffeine to face the day.

She'd waited up as long as she could last night, hoping she'd catch Zach in a better mood and they could begin to hash things out. She couldn't see living in his house with all the tension from the past between them.

Instead, she'd passed out cold, only to come awake in his arms. Her eyelids had been too heavy to stay open but she remembered him kissing her on the lips before she fell asleep again. She didn't think it had been a dream.

"I smell coffee." He entered the kitchen, his chest bare, looking sexy in a pair of gray sweats sitting low on his hips.

Her gaze fell to the muscles he'd lacked as a lanky teen. As she'd thought yesterday, he was built, his chest a buff feast, his pecs defined, a six pack below, and a trail of hair leading... downward to his cock, the outline visible through the soft material.

She glanced up, trying to pretend she hadn't been staring. "Can I get you a cup?" Her voice sounded scratchy to her ears.

"I got it." He walked over and popped in a K-cup. While the single brew machine worked its magic, he stood too close, his freshly showered, masculine scent a reminder that he had carried her to bed last night.

She waited for him to finish and sit down at the granite top kitchen table. Joining him, she stared until he lifted his gaze from his mug. "We need to talk."

He raised an eyebrow.

"Fine. *I* need to talk and I'd appreciate it if you'd listen. It's not enough for me to take advantage of your generosity by giving Dani and me a place to hide out. I want to tell you what happened all those years ago. Even if you don't want to hear it."

"I need to hear it." He rubbed his eyes with the palms of his hand. "I just don't want to." He picked up the mug, took a long sip, placed the drink on the table then leaned against the back of his chair. Arms folded across his chest, his stony gaze met hers. "Let's hear it."

She knew he wouldn't make it easy on her. Despite having been sixteen and life being out of her control, she understood.

Unable to sit still, she rose to her feet and began pacing the kitchen. "Do you remember me telling you about coming home and seeing creepy men meeting with my dad?"

She paused and glanced at him, waiting for a nod before she continued. "It turns out, he was involved with the Mob. After you dropped me off after school that last day, I walked into the house to find the FBI waiting."

A muscle ticked in his jaw, the only outer reaction she'd seen so far.

"They told us we were leaving and I had five minutes to pack a few personal items and we would be disappearing. Witness Protection, they said."

"Holy shit." He shook his head, his eyes wide in obvious shock. "You have no fucking clue how hard I tried to find you. The lengths I went to, the hacking... and you were a ghost. And when you showed up with another name, things started to fall into place."

"Hacking?" she asked, her voice rising. She'd never

want him to get into trouble because of her.

A smirk lifted the corners of his mouth. The man was too damned sexy for his own good. Or hers. "A story for another day. Go on."

"I got hysterical. I didn't want to leave my home, my friends. Most of all, I didn't want to leave you." Her eyes filled at the memory of that awful day. "You can't imagine I'd leave you without a word? We were so close. We understood each other." She'd thought they were soulmates. He'd lost his mother and she had as well. They had a bond.

His jaw tightened and he visibly forced himself to relax. "I thought so too, so let me be clear. I understand why you disappeared," he said slowly, as if choosing his words carefully. "I don't get why you didn't try to reach out and let me know you were okay, before you left. Even if you couldn't explain where you were going, at least I would have had that. You had to know I would lose my mind once I realized you were gone with no word."

She walked back to the table and sat in the seat closest to him. "I did know that. And if I hadn't been so frightened by the agents who escorted us out of the house, I would have. But they told me if I didn't memorize everything, if I opened my mouth, my father would be killed. I was sixteen years old and the kind of kid who did as I was told. When federal agents said my dad would die, and my baby sister was at risk, I believed them."

He stared at her for a few uncomfortable beats. "But eventually? You never thought to reach out? Did you forget about what we shared so easily?"

Though his voice was clipped, she heard the hurt beneath. "Of course not! At first not only was I afraid to defy the agents, but I also thought you'd be safer without me contacting you. If the Mob was after my father, there was no way I wanted to put you in danger."

She rose and began to pace the kitchen.

"My family would have protected me."

"Really?" She raised her eyebrows and shot him a disbelieving look. "It was the *Mob* and you hadn't yet turned eighteen. Money couldn't protect you." She rubbed her hands up and down her arms, remembering those difficult days.

"And later? You certainly thought it was safe enough to show up now."

He wasn't being stubborn, he was revealing his reality. One she hadn't let herself think about too closely or she'd never have stopped crying or gotten out of bed.

She closed her eyes for a brief moment before opening them again. "Haven't you ever reached a point in your life where you think, *it's too late*? If I wanted to have any kind of life, I had to push you out of my mind. *I had no choice.* I didn't use social media, and though I was tempted to borrow my sister's account and look you up, I didn't. Because I had to move forward."

His jaw was still clenched tight but his eyes no longer shot daggers at her. No doubt he'd had to move on too. Something else she hadn't allowed herself to dwell on.

"After I took Dani and we ran, I needed gas and I wanted to load up on food for the trip. We were in line at a rest stop when I saw a magazine and your family was on the cover. At the Cannes Film festival. I couldn't not look so I skimmed the article."

He shook his head. "I hate publicity. The whole blow up after Nikki's mother tried to kill Winter, the hero shit... so not my thing. I don't know how Harrison deals with it, but we went to support his film." His lips lifted and she saw the pride in her eyes for his sibling.

"You are so fortunate to have so many brothers and your sisters." She smiled at him but knew he needed her to finish her story. "Anyway, that article was how I discovered you not only owned the bars but you ran a P.I. business to find missing people. I knew then you could help me. I was already driving east with no idea where to go. Seeing you, reading that... it was like a sign."

She walked over and sat down beside him, covering his tanned, warm hand in hers. "I realize you may never forgive me but at least tell me you understand? I'm grateful enough you're willing to help me but staying here with those walls you put up between us?" She felt the heaviness in her throat and swallowed hard, not wanting to break down in front of him. "It's just... I missed you and I'd like us to at least be friends."

She knew better than to hope for more. He had a life without her, although she wasn't sure if that included a wife or girlfriend. Though she doubted he would have kissed her last night if he had someone in his life. At least, the boy she knew long ago wouldn't have.

And she and her sister had their own lives, too. Dani had school and friends, and Hadley had her students to go home to... assuming she wasn't fired and it ever became safe to return.

Even if a part of her heart would always belong to Zach.

HADLEY'S EXPLANATION MADE perfect sense. All these years, Zach had resented her leaving and not contacting him, thinking he could have protected her, but she was right. Family and money wouldn't have been enough to go up against a threat he probably wouldn't have seen coming. He'd been a skinny kid with impressive computer abilities for his age. It wasn't until she'd disappeared that he'd overhauled his entire persona.

Tired of being made fun of because his girlfriend had disappeared, and the jokes about her not wanting to be with a nerd so she'd had to pack up her whole life and leave, he'd hit the gym. Built up his muscles. And continued to search for Hadley, hanging out in Internet Relay Chat and honing his skills.

But her point was well-taken. The fact that she'd tried to keep him safe went a long way towards smoothing the sharp edges of his anger. When he stopped thinking with his emotions, he knew she had done the right thing by following the FBI's instructions to cut all ties. But that didn't mean he shouldn't keep his walls up and defenses high, for when she eventually left him again. Something she'd already told him she planned to do as soon as her father said it was safe to return.

"Zach?" Her hand was still covering his.

He exhaled a deep breath, feeling his resentment ebb.

"Yeah. Just thinking. It's a lot to process." And he

didn't believe rehashing things would help nor was he ready to explain his past after she'd left. They had time. "I'm working on getting over it," he assured her. "And yes, I understand."

"I'm glad." Her eyes glittered with gratitude.

"How about we go phone shopping?" He changed the subject and she hopped up from her seat.

"Yes! Let me run and get ready."

He nodded, appreciating the break from the intensity of their conversation, and escaped to his bedroom where he changed into a pair of cargo shorts, a T-shirt, and sneakers.

A little while later, she came back into the kitchen wearing black leggings and a matching T-shirt with bright fluorescent colors that said, "Sorry, is my teaching interrupting all your talking?"

He grinned at the saying. "You followed your dream," he said, impressed. "You're a teacher?"

"I am." Her shoulders straightened. "I was able to go to school on loans and qualify for the Teacher Loan Forgiveness Plan."

He nodded. "That's great."

"Except I had to leave without notice, and I'll need to come up with an excuse for missing the last week of school and hope I'm back by the next year. But I'll figure something out."

"Ready to go out?"

"Yes." She pulled the strap of her handbag up on her shoulder. "I just wish I had something better to wear. I packed so quickly, I don't know what I was thinking."

"You weren't thinking, you were panicking." And for the first time, he allowed himself to consider her feelings when he'd dropped her off at home only to find out life as she knew it was over at sixteen years old.

Now it was happening all over again and the least he could do was make things easier. She'd given him more insight that allowed him to lower his walls because he could finally acknowledged she'd suffered too.

She was waiting for a reply about her clothing. He already loved the saying on the shirt. Now he took in the tight fit of her outfit and thought she looked sexy in her clothes. But having sisters and sisters-in-law, he knew women cared more about these things.

"You can always go shopping." As long as she was with him or his family and he felt she was safe.

She parted her lips. "Oh. I appreciate that but I need to find some kind of job to make money under the table before I can afford to go. I'll just make do with what I brought."

He frowned. "You don't need to work, you know. I can help."

"No." She shook her head. "I didn't come here because you have money. I came because you have the skills needed to protect us. Besides, I like to work, and I'm used to keeping busy, even in the summer when teaching is over. It's important to me."

He nodded. It was second nature to him to offer help, either monetarily or with his skills. But he wasn't surprised she turned him down. Even as a teenager, she hadn't liked when he bought her meals, so he'd taken her to less expensive places and insisted he pay on a date, anyway. He already caught a glimpse of her pride yesterday, when she said she'd pay him back for the phones.

He respected her feelings and found her attitude a refreshing change from the women he occasionally dated. "I'm sure we can work something out at the bar."

As in, she'd work, and he'd pay her in cash from his personal money. He wouldn't put the bar at risk by paying her unreported income, but he needed to keep her calm and by his side, not freaking out because he was handing her money.

He wouldn't let her, or Dani put themselves in danger because Hadley felt guilty about accepting handouts.

For now, they had phones to buy and a laptop for him to fix and he was aware she'd fight him on the cost of it all.

Chapter Seven

AFTER A LONG day of shopping, Hadley walked to her room in Zach's house, fell onto the bed, and realized just how damned tired she actually was. For the forty-eight hours she'd been alone with Dani, driving east and staying in crappy motels, she'd woken up at every sound, fear making her heart pound in her chest. Last night, she'd tossed and turned, worrying about Dani, who'd sent Zach one text from Layla's phone.

"Tell Hads, 👍 ."

That was all. *Teenagers,* she thought with a roll of her eyes.

Tonight she and Zach were going to Serenity and Michael's for dinner so Hadley could see her sister, and she was grateful the family had invited her without her having to ask.

She'd left Zach downstairs, turning on their new phones, putting them on his carrier's plan, an argument she'd lost on the way home, and installing VPN to make sure their cell and laptops were untraceable.

Yes, *laptops.* Which brought her to the other reasons she was probably feeling wiped out. Talking about the past this morning had been rough. Then they'd spent two hours in the store quibbling over which phone models were right for her and Dani, only for her to lose the battle. She'd insisted they could live with the least expensive models but even those were beyond her means. Zach had taken her to the Apple store and insisted upon purchasing top of the line phones, maxed out with storage she didn't need.

Then he'd held firm on buying Dani a new laptop because not only was hers old, but the screen had cracks, something he'd seen when he'd inspected the computer last night. As the salesperson called into the back of the store, asking someone to bring out their purchases, he'd told them to make it two, one for her as well.

Short of throwing a tantrum in front of a packed crowd, she'd been forced to accept gracefully and was now worrying about how she was ever going to pay him back. But considering her acceptance was the first time she'd seen a genuine smile from him since she'd arrived, a part of her found it worth swallowing her pride.

Even grumpy and pissed off, he was sexy as hell but when he'd grinned at her? Her panties had nearly melted off. At sixteen, she barely knew what sex was, though she'd planned on giving him her virginity on prom night. But watching him in action and happy?

Her underthings were soaked, her nipples hard, and she knew she was in trouble.

It wasn't easy being in Zach's house and dealing with seeing him again for the first time in years. Sexual attraction was one thing. But she also had so many emotions vying for her attention, she didn't know what to do with them all. And ever present was the fear that had brought her here in the first place.

If she thought she'd be able to nap now, there was no way.

ZACH DROVE THEM to his parents' house in his Mercedes convertible. He pulled up to a gate and punched in a code. After the doors finally opened, they made their way up a tree-lined driveway. His parents had bought the house a year ago, shortly before Zach purchased the second Back Door bar.

They'd wanted a vacation place large enough for their huge family. With Harrison and Winter spending most of their time at their home out here instead of the city and Zach having a place of his own, they purchased a nine bedroom to accommodate the ever-growing family. It had become a second home for everyone that came to visit.

Hadley remained silent on the way here and

though it was a short trip, he sensed she had a lot on her mind.

"Did you nap?" he asked. She'd gone upstairs while he secured Hadley and Dani's new electronics.

She shook her head. "There's just so much going on, my mind is spinning. Oh, wow!" she exclaimed.

"What is it?" he asked, as he parked the car behind other vehicles that told him some of his siblings were here. He shut the engine off, then turned towards her.

"This house. It's gorgeous!"

He glanced at the structure in front of him, seeing it through her eyes. An ocean-front estate, it was a traditional style home with gray shingles and a long white porch. There were blue and white cushions on floating benches attached to the house that he knew his parents loved.

"It is. But it also must be overwhelming for you."

Even back in high school, she'd tiptoe around, intimidated by the size of the house, the fact that there were so many bedrooms, the large pool in the backyard, and the playroom with a pool table and screening room in the basement.

She swallowed hard as she looked at him. "You remember my… insecurities back then?"

He tapped her nose, surprising himself with the easy gesture. "I remember everything about you."

Her eyes glazed with emotion.

He wasn't sure where either his comment or reaction had come from but he liked the intimacy between them.

"You're right though. All this?" She gestured around her. "You can't imagine the tiny house we live in back home."

He tipped his head to the side, studying her. "*We?*"

She nodded. "I live with my dad and Dani." She drew a deep breath and slowly exhaled. "You already know Patrice was a shitty person and mom, even after she had Dani. When we moved to Illinois, it only got worse. She hated being uprooted and she didn't take care of Dani or the house, so I stepped in and took over."

"Jesus, you were only sixteen." He couldn't imagine the burden put on her young shoulders.

"The early days weren't as bad. Once Dani went to kindergarten, which thankfully was a full day, Patrice had too much time on her hands and she used that time to get high." She shook her head, her disgust obvious.

He stretched his arm out over her seat. "So not exactly mother material."

"No. And things only got worse. Time passed, some nights she didn't come home… the one good thing my father did was ensure she lost custody. Now she only sees Dani when one of us is there to supervise. I pretty much raised my sister. There was no way I could move out and leave her to my father's parenting. He might have been around, and he didn't do drugs but Dani needed me."

"You devoted your life to her." She nodded and his admiration for her only grew.

He had the sudden need to be closer and leaned in. His head told him to be careful getting nearer to her but he was following his instincts. Her gaze on his, she met him halfway until their lips were millimeters apart, the attraction and spark between them still hotter than ever.

"Hey! Are you going to sit in the car all night? I'm starving!" Dani's voice had them both jumping back in their respective seats.

Cockblocker, he thought, amused by the teen and also grateful she'd stopped him from acting too quickly. He glanced at Hadley, whose cheeks had turned red. "Come on. Let's go inside."

He climbed out of the car, walked around to her side and opened the door. Extending a hand, he helped her out, her long skirt swaying around her legs. The fabric was made of a crinkly material that made it *too casual* in her eyes, or so she'd told him when he whistled as she'd joined him after her rest upstairs.

Her long, tanned legs looked phenomenal in that skirt and the second he saw her, dirty thoughts of lifting the flimsy material, backing her against the wall and finally, *finally*, driving into her wet heat consumed him. When his cock responded to the vision, he silently counted to ten, knowing he couldn't walk into his parents' house with a hard-on.

Once he'd calmed, he reached into the area behind his seat and pulled out the shopping bag with the goodies he'd brought for Dani. Then he followed Hadley up the walk towards her sister, who waited with Layla. It came as no shock that *his* sister now had a light blue streak in her hair on the same front piece as Dani's. Knowing Serenity, Zach was sure Layla's was washable.

"Looks like they're bonding," Hadley said, and he heard the relief in her voice.

He grasped her hand and squeezed. "Told you she'd be fine."

"Hads!" Dani called, starting towards her sister.

Hadley rushed forward but instead of Dani greeting her, she ran to Zach. "You brought my phone and laptop!" she squealed.

He caught the disappointed look on Hadley's face. Leaning down to Dani, he handed her the bag, and whispered in her ear. "Your sister was with me when we picked the phone and a new laptop."

From the little he'd seen of Dani and Hadley's relationship, there was real love there. He trusted Dani to do the right thing.

Dani ran over to her sister. "Thank you for the new laptop!" she squealed and hugged Hadley, not letting go of the shopping bag. "I love you."

"Ouch but thank you." Hadley rubbed her shoulder but she was smiling. "And I love you, too."

He embraced Layla.

"Dani," he said. "Don't tag your location or take pictures and post them on social media. Nothing that might show your whereabouts."

She nodded. "I promise," she said and the two teens ran off to get Dani's electronics set up and working for her.

Placing his hand on Hadley's back, he led her into the house where he discovered his sister, Jade and her husband, Knox, who held their daughter in the entry.

"I didn't realize this was a big family gathering," Hadley whispered.

"Any invitation has the possibility of being a large Dare get-together." He knew she still wasn't comfortable around everyone and was worried they'd blame her for leaving him. He should have warned her ahead of time but hadn't given it any thought.

Zach held out his hands. "Give me that sweet baby girl," he said, grinning as Knox plunked the ten-month old into his arms.

"Always the baby stealer," Jade said.

Zach opened his mouth to speak but his sister beat him to it. "I know, you're everyone's favorite uncle." She repeated his standard refrain.

Zach kissed her head and inhaled the smell of baby shampoo, aware of Hadley's curious eyes on him the whole time. "Hadley, you remember Jade and in case you didn't meet him the other day in the city, this is her husband, Knox. Knox, this is Hadley Stevens."

Knox extended his hand and Hadley shook it. "Nice to meet you. Jade's told me a lot about you."

"All good I hope?" Hadley's cheeks flushed with embarrassment, and he understood why. She was still waiting to be judged but at least she made a joke and went with the flow.

"All good," Jade assured her. "Aurora and Nick are inside with the kids, and Mom and Dad. Might as well go to the kitchen. I want to give Sage a bottle before dinner."

Zach took the hint and handed the baby back to his sister. Knox put an arm around her shoulder, and they walked towards the kitchen.

"Are you okay?" he asked Hadley. "I should have given you a heads up. You never know who's going to be at one of these dinners."

She treated him to a smile he could tell was forced. "Everyone's been lovely so far. I'm sure everything will be okay." He did his best not to wince because that sounded like *famous last words.*

HADLEY SAT AROUND a large table surrounded by Zach's family. The pit in her stomach was deep but she knew the issues were her own. Nobody in this room had made her feel unwelcome. She just wasn't used to being with people she still felt as if she'd wronged. Nor was she used to a large, warm family or a formal dining area. Not that she could call this gathering formal.

Everyone talked over each other, asking questions loudly and laughing at their answers. Even her sister seemed to fit right in, and Hadley envied the lack of self-consciousness possessed by teenagers. She smiled, watching Dani so at ease.

"Hey, you're awfully quiet," Zach said, whispering in her ear from his seat beside her.

She lifted her shoulder closest to him. "Just observing."

Beneath the table, he slid his hand over her thigh and clasped her hand in his, squeezing for reassurance. Her skin beneath the soft cotton fabric of her skirt tingled from his body heat and so did her sex.

"So Hadley, how do you like Zach's Hamptons house?" Aurora asked.

"It's beautiful. Just like this one. You all have such wonderful decorative taste," she said, aware Serenity was listening.

A little squeak sounded from the baby monitor on the table and all four parents turned towards the noise.

Though Aurora's daughter, Leah, sat between both parents, both babies, Aurora and Jade's, were sleeping in separate pack and plays in a nearby room. When the peep didn't turn into a wail, the parents seemed to relax.

"Well," Serenity said, a smile on her face, "We have a decorator in the family and another friend who's in the business as well."

Hadley raised her eyebrows. "Who?"

"Chloe Kingston is a friend of the family and she helped us with this house. I wanted it to have country charm with modern amenities. And we have a cousin in the city, Lucy Dare, who also works with a design firm. I give her the more modern designs." Serenity lifted her glass and took a sip of water. "Spread the wealth so no one is offended."

And that was how Hadley remembered Serenity. A genuine person who cared about others. Although she hadn't seen Serenity in a long time, she still looked young and beautiful, her dark hair now cut to shoulder length.

"That sounds like the perfect dichotomy."

"It is," Aurora said. "Hadley, Jade and I are going shopping one day this week. While we're in town, I figured we could pick up some summer clothes. Zach mentioned you might need some things. Would you like to join us? It'll be fun."

Hadley turned and shot Zach a questioning look. He held up both hands, an adorably sheepish look on his face. "I might have mentioned it."

That, he would pay for. She pressed her palms against her eyes, hoping she didn't get a headache. As much as she didn't want to be indebted to him or have him think she was using him for his money, she *did* need clothing. Just some pieces that she'd forgotten.

It was hard to accept. She'd been independent her entire life, more so for the last ten years, earning her own money, taking care of her sibling and the house. To Hadley, being reliant on someone else put her at a disadvantage when she knew she needed the ability to run if the need arose. She didn't know how to accept help. But right now, she needed to and she was grateful for the offer.

She removed her hands and glanced at his sisters. "I'd like that. Thank you. For some reason I dumped my entire lingerie drawer into my suitcase and not much more." She shook her head and her face flushed. "Even this skirt and top were in there."

"I know what's in that drawer and it's mostly bras,

panties and her vibrator," Dani said to Layla, speaking too loudly.

"What do you know about vibrators?" The words flew out of Hadley's mouth.

"I'm almost fourteen, not three, you know." Between both Hadley and her sister, her cheeks flamed in mortification while everyone at the table did their best to hide their chuckles.

"Someone please shoot me," she muttered, covering her face with her hands.

Zach laughed but his hand slid to her thigh and stayed there.

The vibrator conversation broke whatever tension that Hadley had been feeling and she enjoyed his family and the rest of the meal along with the company.

After dinner, Serenity suggested Hadley and Dani spend some alone time and Hadley was only too happy to take Zach's mom up on the offer. She and Dani took a walk around the private property surrounding the house. Between the fresh ocean air, the knowledge that she was safe, and the half hour alone with her sister, Hadley felt like a weight had been lifted off her chest, and she had Zach and his family to thank.

She left the house feeling lighter than she had in… months. Since before her father started bringing strange men to their home. Maybe even longer. By the time she said goodbye to Zach's family, she was calmer and less stressed.

And her focus was on Zach and his touches at the table. Casual to outsiders but intimate to her.

★　★　★

ZACH SENSED THE difference in Hadley on the drive back to his house. Being with his family had soothed instead of stressed her more, and he was grateful to them for making her feel welcome. If she was going to be here for a while, there was no reason for there to be tension. He noticed the difference in himself, too. His anger at her had dissipated and he was more open to getting to know her again with the qualifying fact that he knew she would leave again when the time came. No surprises.

Once home, they walked inside. He locked up and set the alarm.

"I'm going to turn in. I'm exhausted," Hadley said. "But thank you for tonight. Your family is incredible. The closeness, the laughter, it was great."

He caught the twinge of sadness in her voice that was no doubt caused by the lack of the same in her family, or with her parents, at least. "You and Dani share the same thing. Speaking of Dani…"

"Nope. Don't go there." Hadley held up a hand

and shook her head. Once again, her cheeks flamed with embarrassment, turning a healthy shade of red.

He chuckled. "I was going to say, speaking of Dani, she's pretty grown up for her age. That's why she and Layla get along so well."

"Oh. I thought you meant… Well, never mind."

He stepped closer, inhaling her soft floral scent. "I know what you thought, and I'll admit, I wouldn't mind knowing more about that vibrator you have in your room."

Because if he'd been hard after the near kiss in the car, the thought of Hadley using a sex toy while under his roof had desire racing through his veins.

"Zach," she said on a shaky exhale.

The sound of his name on her lips called to something primal inside him and he stepped forward, slid a hand behind her neck and pulled her to him, sealing his lips over hers. She moaned and softened against him, wrapping her arms around his neck and falling into the kiss.

Their tongues tangled, and since she'd eaten a mint on the drive home, the fresh cooling flavor hit him first. But the longer they stood making out like teenagers, the warmer her mouth became and he couldn't deny that exploring the deep recesses felt like coming home. He could kiss her forever. Hooking an arm around her waist, he pulled her against him, his hard cock rubbing against her soft skirt.

The desire to pull up the flimsy material was strong. She was everything he wanted, desired and had missed. Letting himself admit his feelings had the potential to destroy the barriers he'd erected at a time when he needed to reinforce them. Before he crossed that final line.

She pushed his shoulders and broke the kiss, surprising him. "We shouldn't," she said through well-kissed lips.

He breathed in deep, doing his best to calm his breathing... and his erection. She was right but he didn't like her being the one to end things. "Why not?"

She sighed. "I just think our timing is off."

"Our timing is *always* off." Why was he digging in to argue when she had a point?

"Zach, yesterday you could barely look at me. You might be more understanding today, but I don't want you to have any regrets. Besides, we don't know each other anymore." Her voice shook and he recognized the wariness and fear in her tone.

He had only himself to blame and no choice but to accept the truth. He'd been the one to put up the walls between them. Could he get to know her again and still protect himself from the inevitable?

"Is that what you want? To get to know me again?" Though he wondered if she had someone waiting for her at home, he wasn't ready to ask. Unable to stop himself, he brushed his knuckles down her cheek.

"Of course, I do." She smoothed her trembling hands on her skirt. "I missed you. But I also know how things end. I have a job and life back home and I'm leaving when this mess with my father is over."

She hadn't said anything he didn't already know. Hadn't already warned himself about. But hearing her say it was a stab wound to his heart.

Chapter Eight

A FEW DAYS passed since Hadley had pulled back from kissing Zach and though she had major regrets, she also knew she'd done the right thing. As much as *she* wanted him, diving into bed when just the day before he'd been giving her the cold shoulder was not the way to go. Besides, she knew how easily she could fall for him again and since she wasn't here for good, she needed to be careful.

Since that night, Zach had spent many hours at the bar due to the inventory issues and he promised he'd work with his manager on giving her a shift once he sorted things out. Which meant right now she had no spending money.

Yet here she was, with Aurora and Jade, in an upscale department store. Despite wanting to be able to pay for herself, she accepted Zach's credit card because she truly did need clothes. She would have preferred a less expensive place to shop but his sisters weren't aware of Hadley's financial issues and insisted on a girls-day mall outing.

She did her best to hit the sale racks and buy easily washable items. She found two black leggings, one pair of denim shorts, tank tops and two summer dresses. When Aurora insisted on checking out the shoe department, Hadley ended up with wedge sandals and a pair of flipflops.

Now they were all sitting at a round table at the Neiman Marcus restaurant. One look at the prices and she reached for the water, taking a sip out of the glass, otherwise she might groan out loud.

"I am so glad to be out with you both," Jade said. "Serenity is taking Sage overnight so when I come home I can nap. And later on, Knox and I can be alone." Her eyes glittered with love for her husband.

"And Melanie has Leah and Ellie," Aurora said of her surrogate mom. She leaned back in her seat, her smile as wide as Jade's. "We are owed that after Leah walked in on us a couple of weeks ago." Her face flushed pink. "So mortifying. Nick mumbled something about mommy not feeling well and daddy taking care of her and promised we'd be right out. At least the covers were half up."

"Eew. Don't give me that visual of my brother." Jade wrinkled her nose in disgust.

Hadley choked on her water, laughing.

"Just you wait, Hadley," Aurora said to her. "One day you'll have kids and know exactly what I mean." Her sweet grin was infectious.

Hadley shook her head. "I'm busy enough with a

nosey teenage sister and my high school students."

"You never know. I didn't think I would have kids," Jade said, sobering. "I thought my mom's health issues would be mine, as well."

Hadley knew all about their mom Audrey's mental health issues, but she wasn't sure how it had affected Jade. Nor did she think it was her place to ask.

"Anyway," Jade continued. "Then Knox and his potent sperm came along and voila! I got pregnant, which forced me to face my feelings." She picked up a popover and broke it in half, the steam billowing from the delicious-looking pastry.

"You two are so… open!" Hadley envied their closeness. She hoped that when Dani grew up, they'd share a similarly tight relationship.

Jade lifted a shoulder. "We're family. And the women in this family are close. Which brings me to you and Zach."

Aurora winced. "Not smooth."

"Fine, I'll get to the point. We hope you and Zach can rekindle your relationship. I know things were awkward at first but I saw glimpses of my old brother that night at dinner." She leaned closer to Hadley. "And I know we have you and your return to thank. He missed you so much."

Hadley wrapped her hands around the glass and tried to figure out how to explain things to these well-meaning women who only wanted the best for their brother. "I realize my leaving was painful and the lack of communication was even worse for him. It was awful for me too and I was in a new state and school where I didn't know a soul."

"That must have been so hard," Aurora whispered.

"It was, but not as rough as you had it." Hadley wouldn't begin to compare.

Aurora had grown up in foster care, aged out and gotten pregnant after a no-names exchanged, one-night stand with Nick. Unfortunately, she'd found out she was having his baby after he'd left, and they'd coincidentally and fortunately, reunited five years later. Her early life hadn't been easy and if anyone could understand a scary, unfamiliar situation, it was Aurora.

"Don't do that," Aurora said, shaking her head. "Everyone's hard time is theirs. No need to minimize your own."

Hadley nodded in understanding. "Anyway, I've explained to Zach all about my past and why I didn't keep in touch and I think he's coming to terms with what happened."

She wouldn't mention their kiss or the fact that he'd definitely *seemed* to have come around. Either that or he was in deep denial, and he'd eventually explode with anger. Who knew?

"He seems lighter," Aurora murmured.

"Not to mention my brother hasn't had a real relationship since you."

Hadley jerked in her seat and her breath left her in a rush. "That's not possible."

"But it is. Don't get me wrong, there have been women in his life, but there has never been anyone he's brought to a family dinner." Jade lifted her napkin and placed the linen square on her lap. "Hand to God," she said, raising her palm forward. "Hookups have been more his thing."

Something she had no desire to hear about.

Hadley shook out her napkin and placed it on her thighs. "Just another way I messed up his life."

"Or he knew he already found the one and nobody else would do," Aurora said.

These women were relentless. Hadley couldn't deny she was shocked to hear Zach hadn't had a relationship since they'd been together. Neither had she. As much as her heart liked the romantic idea of a second chance, she had obligations, both to the school and with the loan agreement tying her to another state.

Hadley glanced at them. "Listen, don't get your hopes up. Zach and I really don't know each other anymore, and when my problems are resolved, I have to go back to Illinois." She repeated what she'd told Zach because she didn't want them to be disappointed.

Aurora and Jade met each other's gazes. "We'll see," Jade said, just as the waiter made his way to their table.

The rest of the meal was light and filled with girl talk Hadley didn't often get to enjoy. Another thing she'd miss when it was time to go home. But for right now, both she and her sister were safe and that was what mattered.

ZACH GLANCED AT Maddox. "You're telling me more liquor bottles are missing?" Zach asked.

Maddox shook his head. "I don't understand it. The counts are right when everything comes in."

Running a hand through his hair, Zach studied the bar and the short hall leading to the storage room and offices. Before he could think on it further, the door opened and Hadley walked in, shopping bags in her hands. The sight of her distracted him, his gaze falling on her navy leggings and form-fitting lavender tank top that accentuated her curves.

"I'll be in the offices," Maddox said as Zach made his way towards Hadley.

"Here, let me take those." He reached out and unloaded her burden. "Glad to see you and the girls did well."

"Too well." She wrinkled her nose, an adorably cute expression he'd always loved watching her make. "They're master shoppers, well… Jade is. Aurora's less comfortable which made me feel better." She drew a breath. "Listen, I realize this looks like I bought a ton of things but most were on sale and I'm keeping an itemized list of everything you've paid for. I promise I will–"

He placed his finger over her lips, his skins sizzling at the light touch. "Stop worrying about it. I won't miss it. And I know that only makes you feel worse but it's the truth. I don't want you adding to your stress."

"You're right. It doesn't make me feel better. But thank you."

"You're welcome." He met her gaze, wanting her to see the sincerity in his.

With her bags in one hand, he wrapped an arm around her shoulder and led her to the bar. "Jade and Aurora dropped you off?"

She nodded. "They have the night alone with their husbands and couldn't wait to get back."

"Aah, the grandmothers are babysitting," he mused aloud. "Mom loves it." He walked over to one of the servers who was standing near a pillar, standing by until a table of customers decided what they wanted to order. "Can you put this in the office, Deke?"

The other man nodded. "You got it, Zach."

"Thank you." Zach handed him the shopping bags. Turning to Hadley, he gestured to the empty bar stools. "Have a seat."

She pulled out a chair and settled onto the seat.

"Want something to drink?"

She shook her head. "No, thanks. I'm floating from all the club soda I drank at lunch."

He chuckled. "I'm sure. Will you be okay here? I need to go make a couple of calls. I'll be back in a few minutes and we can head out."

"Take your time. I could have had the girls drop me off at your house, but I wanted to talk to you about me working here." She glanced up at him with wide eyes.

He never could resist her. Though he'd prefer she not worry about money, he admired her pride and work ethic. Besides, if he gave her a job, she'd be with him all day and he wouldn't worry about her being alone.

He'd already hired Alpha to keep an eye on her father and anyone he was associating with but that didn't mean anything for Hadley and Dani.

There was no need for her to know.

"Zach?" Hadley waved a hand in front of his face. "I asked you about a job."

He shook his head to clear his thoughts. "Right. I'll

introduce you to Maddox when I'm finished with my calls and we'll find a place for you."

Her shoulders visibly relaxed at his reply. "Thank you."

"Anything for you," he said, winking at her and walking away before he could catalogue her response.

Chapter Nine

HADLEY GLANCED AROUND the bar. It was open for business but as it was only three p.m., the tables and stools were mostly empty. Hushed murmurs of employees sounded around her. Instead of letting her mind wander, she kept her focus on the here and now, and the basic running and set up before things got busy.

A dark-haired man stepped behind the bar and shot her a charming smile. "Hi. Can I get you a drink?" he asked, picking up a cardboard coaster and sliding it across the bar.

She'd said no to Zach but changed her mind. "Sure. I'll take a club soda or seltzer."

"Sure thing." He scooped ice into a glass followed by filling it with the soda gun. "Here you go. I'm Maddox, the manager," he said, treating her to a friendly smile. "I saw you come in with the boss."

She nodded. "Nice to meet you. I'm Hadley."

Maddox glanced over her shoulder and groaned. "Oh shit," he muttered.

"What's wrong?" Hadley asked.

"My brother's guidance counselor is here and her

showing up is never a good thing," he muttered, just as a woman sat down a few seats down from Hadley and Maddox strode over.

"Hello, Mr. James," she said.

"Ms. Connelly. Is my brother okay?" he asked in a rush.

"Yes, of course. Joe is fine or I would have called your work number. I did try your cell phone but it went to voice mail and I left a message."

"I was tied up with a problem."

She nodded. "I understand. As you know, I normally ask parents or guardians to come see me at school, but I pass by here on the way home and thought we could talk."

Hadley peeked at the woman from the side. A petite red-head, she leaned an arm on the bar, not seeming intimidated by Maddox, who'd crossed both of his arms across his chest.

"What did my brother do that has you making a house-call?" he asked, his voice and stiff demeanor no longer as welcoming as it had been earlier.

"It's more like a work-call," she said, lifting her lips in a smile that wasn't returned. Knowing her joke fell flat, she cleared her throat. "You're aware your brother is struggling in school but he failed his last English test. His teacher is willing to let him retake it before final grades are turned in so he has the opportunity to pass for the year. He failed to show up during lunch today for the test."

Although Hadley shouldn't eavesdrop, she couldn't help but overhear.

"Dammit." Maddox ran a hand through his hair and began pacing behind the bar.

"Joe promised he'd retake the test and tell you. He's done neither. I have a soft spot for struggling students and Joe is a good kid. I convinced his teacher to give him one more opportunity next week. That gives him study time. I was hoping if you spoke to him…"

"He'll be there. And he'll study ahead of time. Please email me the day, time and place. I'll walk him in myself."

Ms. Connelly nodded. "I knew you'd say that. You've been doing the best you can since he's come to live with you and he's lucky to have an older sibling who cares." She stood. "Thank you for your time," she said, and walked away.

Every word the woman spoke had resonated with Hadley and as an educator, she couldn't help but respond to Maddox's frustrated look and the caring woman who'd stopped by.

"Maddox?"

He turned to face her, a muscle throbbing in his temple. "I didn't intend to listen, but I couldn't help but overhear. If you don't mind me asking, how old is your brother?"

"Seventeen. My brother got in with the wrong crowd and I said he could finish his senior year here. I figured with him away from the kids causing trouble, he'd get his act together but it's been rough."

She nodded in understanding. "It just so happens I'm an English teacher. I could tutor him this week before his test. I mean, if you want me to."

He blinked, light coming back into his eyes. "Hell, yes. Are you sure?"

"I need something to do. I'm here… visiting Zach but I want to keep busy." She didn't see any reason to bring this man into her drama.

"I can't thank you enough. He gets out at 3:05 and I can have him here by 3:30. It's pretty quiet at this hour. Would you be able to work with him at a corner table? This way I know he shows up and you aren't wasting time waiting for him."

"What's going on?" Zach asked, coming up behind Hadley and putting a hand on her shoulder. Her skin tingled where his calloused hand touched.

She tipped her head back, looking up at him for a brief moment before he stepped beside her.

"Joe's counselor came by to let me know not only is he in danger of failing English but he bailed on a chance to retake a test that would fix things," Maddox muttered. He ran a frustrated hand through his dark hair.

"I offered to tutor him for the next week," she said to Zach.

"As long as you don't mind giving up a corner table for them?" Maddox asked.

Zach nodded. "That's no problem." He looked at Hadley. "You don't mind?"

She shook her head. "I would love to do it."

"Thank you." The relief in Maddox's tone was evident. "When I offered to let him come live with me, I thought he'd get his shit together, not deliberately screw up."

Hadley met his gaze. "Don't feel bad. It's the age. He'll keep testing you, but boundaries and rules aren't a bad thing. It shows him you care."

"Yeah." He blew out a rough breath. "And whatever you charge for tutoring is fine."

Hadley smiled. "It works well for me, too. I need to make spare cash," she said pointedly.

Meeting her gaze, Maddox winked. "Works for me."

"We should get going," Zach said, his hand immediately landing on her shoulder again.

She liked the feel of his possessive touch too much.

"What about my shopping bags?"

He helped her up from her seat. "I already had them put in my trunk."

She ought to be annoyed with his possessiveness but a part of her liked the fact that he could be jealous. Knowing she could affect him after all these years meant something to her. She knew a long-term relationship wasn't possible but could she lay out parameters so they both knew what to expect? Could she be with him knowing the end would come? If she didn't, she would live with even more regrets.

With that in mind, she stood and followed him out of the bar.

HADLEY WAS QUIET on the way home but Zach didn't need conversation. He had plenty on his mind. All that talk about tutoring brought up memories of meeting her for the first time. They'd been in the school library where he'd been sent to tutor her. Friendship came first, then a summer passed, and she'd returned to school with longer hair, fuller breasts and killer curves. He'd really *noticed* her then. Turned out she'd already had a crush on him and everything between them changed.

Just like things had changed again now. She wasn't Mia, she was Hadley and she wasn't *his*. She'd made her feelings clear when she'd backed away the other night. It was too soon. Or maybe she no longer wanted him the same way she once did.

He'd been lost in those memories, those feelings when he'd seen Maddox wink at his girl and he'd been pissed. And jealous. The latter not an emotion he was used to feeling. He needed space to clear his mind because he'd almost bitten off his manager's head for being friendly. Zach parked the vehicle inside his garage and Hadley climbed out before he could help her. Grabbing the bags from the back, he carried them inside, walking through the house and going straight to her bedroom.

Hadley hadn't been in his home for long but her sweet scent permeated the air and that warm, familiar feeling stirred his blood. He needed to get out of here before he did something stupid, like pulling her into another hot kiss. He placed her bags on the floor and turned to leave.

"Are you still upset?" she asked, the question stopping him and she walked around him to enter the bedroom.

He glanced back at her as she plopped down on the bed, bouncing as she did.

He closed his eyes against the vision of her breasts bobbing beneath her tank top, opening his eyelids again when he thought it was safe.

Except she now sat on the bed, knees crossed, her eyelids low, a seductive look on her beautiful face. "Well?" she asked.

He spun back towards her. "I'm not upset, I'm—"

"Jealous?" she asked in a husky voice, her lips glistening with gloss she'd reapplied in the car.

He blinked in surprise. Had he been that obvious?

He did a quick study of her features and saw a teasing smile lifting her lips. This wasn't the same woman who'd pulled away a few nights ago, and if she wanted to tease him, he could play the same game.

"And if I was?" He walked over to where she sat on the bed and looked down into her light blue eyes, bracing one hand on the wooden headboard behind her.

She lifted one shoulder. "I'd say you didn't need to be."

He knew there'd been other men just like he'd been with other women but no one had meant anything to him. "There's no one you left behind at home?" His heart squeezed in his chest as he waited for her answer.

She shook her head. "No relationships for me, either."

He cocked an eyebrow. Damn the women in his family and their big mouths. But he didn't give a shit what Hadley knew about his lack of a romantic past.

Not when she was admitting hers had been similar.

Her tongue slid over her lower lip and that seductive move cut the leash that had tethered him. He bent down and his mouth met hers, their tongues coming together, a prelude to easing the need spiraling through him. She hooked an arm around his neck and using him as an anchor, pulled herself to a sitting position, her lips never leaving his.

But her hands were busy reaching for the hem of his shirt. To help her, he broke the kiss and yanked the collar, pulling his shirt off and tossing it onto the floor.

"Zach." She spoke his name on an awed whisper as she placed her palms on his chest.

He cupped her face in his hands. "We have so much time to make up for."

"But we only have now. Until I can safely take my sister home. Then we go our separate ways."

Everything in him rebelled at her words but he understood them, too. And needed to keep them in mind no matter what happened while she was here. "But I reserve the right to try and change your mind," he said, and cut off conversation by sealing his lips over hers. It wasn't that he was giving her his heart again, but he'd be a fool not to try for more.

Once he was certain she was lost in the kiss, he slid his hands beneath her tank top. "Take it off," he said against her mouth.

He raised his head and she stripped off her top, leaving her in a pink lace bra that pushed up her breasts, exposing tantalizing mounds of flesh.

"Beautiful," he said, dipping his head and pressing a kiss over the soft skin on each. Then he placed his hands behind her back and unhooked the garment, watching as she shimmied the straps down and off her arms, her breasts bobbing with the movement.

He cupped them in his hands and she arched into him. "Feels so good." She moaned the words, tipping back her head, revealing her slender neck.

"I can make you feel even better." He dipped his fingers into the waistband of her pants and she raised her hips, helping him as he pulled off her leggings, taking her panties along with them. He dropped the remainder of her clothes onto the floor.

He stared at her glistening sex, his cock pulsing hard against his jeans. "Fuck. You're so wet," he said, meeting her hazy gaze.

"I've been waiting for you a long time." Her voice hitched and she shook her head, as if she could remove the memories of their separation.

He didn't want to think about it either. "Put your legs on my shoulders and let me devour you."

She positioned herself on the mattress and leaned back, her long legs coming to rest on either side of his head. Without waiting, he knelt and gripped her thighs before dipping his head and swiping his tongue over her pussy, indulging in his first taste. And it was his first taste of her, as they'd done a lot of kissing, fondling, and dry humping as teens rather than taking this step.

Prom night had held so much promise. He closed his eyes and it was his turn to shake off those thoughts and focus on his girl. It was how he'd thought of her then. How he wanted to think of her now.

He swiped his tongue over her again, taking in her honeyed taste, and got back to work.

Chapter Ten

ZACH WAS A master with his tongue, Hadley thought, and it wasn't long before his determined and talented abilities had waves of pleasure washing over her. He worked one long finger inside her as he flickered his tongue over her clit. Pulsing need shot through her and she raised her hips, grinding herself into his mouth.

The rough stubble on his cheek abraded her sensitive flesh in the most delicious of ways. He pulled his finger out and when he returned, there were two digits filling her.

"Zach, please. I need to come." Her hips rolled as she sought out her release.

"Whatever you need." He curled those fingers inside her and rubbed against the spot no man had ever found before.

She saw stars and when his tongue flattened against her clit, he sent her soaring. "Oh God. I'm coming." Her body trembled and she rubbed her pussy against his mouth.

At her words, he doubled down, rubbing faster inside her and devouring her, the sounds he made as erotic as the orgasm crashing through her. As the waves subsided, she pulled at his hair, urging him to stop, her body was too sensitive from his ministrations.

He stood and gazed at her. His mouth glistened with her juices and his eyes were glazed with desire. He unbuttoned his jeans, unzipped them, and pulled them off. His underwear went with them. And there he was, his cock thick and hard, ready to take her.

"Shit," he muttered, wrapping his hand around his cock and pumping it twice as he groaned. "No condoms."

She pushed herself up on her elbows. "None in your bedroom?" she asked.

He shook his head and relief poured through her. "So is it because you ran out? Or—"

"I don't bring women home with me." His sexy lips lifted in a grin. "Except you."

"Because I'm already staying here."

He shook his head. "Because you're you."

His words took her off guard, but she couldn't deny they touched her heart. And despite trying to keep her walls up around him, she wanted what they should have had. What had been stolen from them.

She held out her hands and he grasped them as if they were a lifeline. "Do I need a condom?" he asked in a gruff voice.

"No. I get a shot." And she'd had one about a month before she'd been forced to leave home. "I haven't been with anyone in a long time and I've had my yearly exam. I'm clean."

He set his jaw, a muscle ticking before he obviously forced himself to relax. "I won't ask how long it's been for you. But it's the same for me. It's been a while and I'm also clean."

Her eyes filled, the sudden rush of emotion taking her by surprise.

"What's wrong?"

"This conversation. The fact that we had to have it at all." She swallowed over the lump in her throat.

He sighed. "Yeah. Well, we can't change the past." He pulled her up and kissed her long and hard, the arousal that had ebbed after her orgasm returning.

He cupped her breasts in his hands, tweaking her nipples with his thumb and forefinger, causing her sex to pulse and wetness to seep out of her. "I need you, Zach." For tonight, she would admit her weakness when it came to this man.

Grasping his cock in his hand, he rubbed himself against her slick folds, then set himself at her entrance. His gaze met hers, ensnaring her. She couldn't tear her eyes from his handsome face as he pushed himself inside her.

His thickness stretched her and then he took a final thrust. Though she'd imagined being with Zach, nothing came close to reality as his body filled hers. He was everything she'd dreamed and more.

He reached out a hand and wiped a tear with his finger, his questioning gaze on hers.

"You should have been my first," she whispered. And the fact that he wasn't hurt in ways she'd pushed aside since she'd been forced to leave.

He touched his forehead to hers. "*This* is our first time. We can talk about the past later. Okay?" Before she could reply, he began to move, showing her what she'd been missing.

He slid out and back in, repeating the motion, circling his hips as he thrust inside her, creating a rhythm all their own.

"Oh God, Zach, you feel so good."

"So do you," he said, a muscle ticking in his jaw that told her he was holding back, the sensual glide in and out, deliberately slow.

Her body felt delicious but incomplete. "Harder. I won't break."

His gaze locked on hers.

"I mean it," she said, and her words freed him, each thrust harder than the last, as if imprinting himself on her for all time, giving her exactly what she'd asked for. What she needed.

He pounded into her, grinding his hips with each

successive plunge home. Her body began to tingle, the welcoming feeling of warmth and pleasure consuming her and she flew over the edge, coming hard as he continued the exquisite assault she'd demanded.

★   ★   ★

ZACH WATCHED HADLEY, her orgasm overtaking her. When he was sure she was through, he slowed his pace so she could catch her breath.

Her eyes opened and a slow smile lifted her lips.

"You're beautiful when you come," he said and slipped a hand between them. He slid his fingers over her clit and she moaned, her inner walls squeezing his dick tighter. "Fuck," he bit out, pleasure like he'd never felt before rushing through him. He clenched his teeth, determined not to let go yet. "I'm going to make you come again. With me this time."

"Someone's pretty sure of themselves." She said, her lips curving upward, her cheeks flushed from her earlier climax.

A climax *he'd* given her and he wasn't finished. "I guess I need to prove myself."

He flicked his fingers over her sensitive clit and she arched against his hand, her moan his undoing. Raising his hips, he began to thrust into her, losing himself in the woman he never thought he'd see again.

The woman he'd never let go of in his heart.

"Yes, Zach. More," she said, her nails digging into his shoulders as her body shook beneath his.

Pleasure threatened to detonate inside him and he wanted her along for the ride. Clenching his jaw, he pulled out of her warmth and rubbed his hard cock along her slippery folds.

"Zach!" She shattered, her entire body seizing, as the pressure of his erection took her over and into another climax.

Without waiting, he surged into her again and pumped his hips, the force of his thrusts shaking the bed. His balls drew up and a warning tingle ran along his spine. Arching her hips, their bodies collided and blackness surrounded him as he came.

Awareness returned, his muscles still shaking as he pulled out of her heat. Instead of leaving the bed like he'd done with other women in the past, he pulled Hadley into him and wrapped her in his arms. Because if he was learning anything about her, he sensed she was working herself into a panic about now.

"Umm… we should–"

"Stay just like this," he said.

She pushed out of his embrace and turned to face him. "How about we shower and then we can cuddle?" She touched his cheek and rolled to climb out of bed.

Apparently, she could still surprise him. "A shower sounds good."

A few minutes later, they stood under the spray in the huge stone-tiled shower. "This bathroom is incredible," she said, glancing around at the multiple shower jets on the walls, and the square rain shower head on top.

She tilted her neck so she faced the ceiling and let the water sluice over her face. He'd never seen a more beautiful sight. Picking up the shower gel, he poured a dollop into his palms and rubbed them together. Then, he slid his hands over her shoulders, working the foam over her skin.

"This is such a luxurious treat," she murmured as he knelt and worked his way up one leg at a time, pausing to slide his soapy fingers through her folds. He imprinted the sight of her in his mind, wanting the visual there forever.

She grasped his shoulders, holding on for the ride as he toyed with her clit until a low moan escaped her throat. He glanced up in time to see her entire body tremble as she came apart, his name on her lips.

He rose to his feet and sealed his mouth over hers, wanting everything she could give. She wrapped her arms around his neck, kissing him back, ignoring the water now rushing over them both.

He lifted her and she jumped into his arms, wrapping herself around him. He turned her back to the wall, slamming inside her over and over.

"Oh God. Yes, Zach. More."

As if he planned on stopping. He already knew he wouldn't last long and needed to quicken her pace. Having learned how to send her flying, he slid his hand between them and pressed his thumb long and hard against her clit, waiting for her to tighten around him. And when she came, he followed her over.

Chapter Eleven

Hadley lay in Zach's arms, totally sated and at peace, something she shouldn't be given the state of her life. She blew out a heavy breath and pushed those negative thoughts away.

"Why the sigh? Regrets already?" he asked, his voice clipped.

She slid a hand over his chest, resting her palm against his warm skin. "No. Of course not." She inhaled his woodsy scent and closed her eyes, wishing with everything in her they could have a future. "I'm just being... wistful."

He covered her hand with his. "It's hard, knowing what could have been."

"It is. But I *would* like to know more about you and what happened after I left."

"You mean how did I deal with being the guy whose date disappeared instead of going to prom with him?"

Unexpected tears pooled in her eyes. "I'm so sorry."

"It was a long time ago."

But he hadn't gotten over it. The tightness in his

voice told her as much. If she had to guess, despite his forgiveness and them sleeping together, it still stung. Since there was nothing she could do to change things, she decided to keep the conversation going.

"Tell me about your life, Zach."

He pushed himself up against the pillows and she did the same. She curled her legs beneath her, pulled the sheet over her breasts and settled in to listen.

"Honestly? Life after you left sucked." He clenched and unclenched his fists.

The memories clearly hurt and watching his pain was excruciating. She rubbed her chest, reminding herself she'd asked for the story.

He cleared his throat. "You already know my mother left us when I was four and died by suicide later. I told myself that I don't remember her and I had Serenity to fill the gap... but after you left, I felt her loss more acutely. On top of you leaving, it was unbearable and I needed a distraction."

His words felt like a punch in the stomach but she remained silent. He needed to tell the story his own way.

"So I dove further into computers. Hacking became my favorite pastime. Not that I was able to track you down." He frowned, then reached for a bottle of water on the nightstand, pausing to take a long sip.

After he put the bottle back, he continued.

"I also began bulking up because at some point, I wanted to be able to nail anyone who made fun of me."

She managed a smile. "You certainly accomplished that goal." Reaching out, she squeezed his bicep. "Sexy."

His eyes darkened. "Do not tempt me unless you don't want me to finish the story."

"I definitely want you to finish. Then I want you."

She loved the low growl that reverberated in his chest. "Anyway, by the time summer ended and it was time for college, I'd bulked up and I couldn't fucking wait to get away."

"Did you go to Columbia?" She remembered how excited he'd been when he'd been accepted in April. They were so excited because while she'd be finishing high school, he wouldn't be far away. At the time, they'd been looking towards the future.

He nodded. "That's where I met Remy. We were roommates and bonded immediately. He had a rebellious streak like mine and when I told him about you, he agreed to help me dig for information. Fortunately, or unfortunately, depending on your perspective, we got caught trying to hack into a federal database."

She gasped and grabbed his wrist. "What happened?" The more she heard about his behavior after her disappearance, the worse she felt.

"The feds showed up on our respective doorsteps while we were home for Thanksgiving break. I didn't even know if the database we'd been trying to get into had the information I needed. Given what happened to you, it's doubtful."

"Oh, Zach." Her actions, although she'd been forced to leave him, had defined his life in unimaginable ways.

He met her gaze but instead of pain, she was surprised to see amusement in the dark blue depths. "It's okay. That was the *unfortunate* part. The *fortunate* part was we didn't end up in jail. They offered us a deal. Work for them doing shit I can't reveal because it was part of the agreement we made, and we could stay in school. Nothing would be on our records."

She blew out a long, relieved breath. "You got lucky." He could have ended up in prison for God knew how long.

"More than you know. During those years, Remy and I made contacts, and in our spare time, we developed anti-hacking software that we sold for enough money that I haven't needed to dip into my Dirty Dare Spirits money, *or* the family trust."

She blinked, completely floored by the information and at a loss for words.

"Cat got your tongue?" he asked wryly.

She nodded. "You're amazing."

He winked. "Glad you think so." He sobered then, his mouth pulling into a firm line.

"What is it?"

"Part of the deal I made with the feds was that I stop hacking, which meant I stopped searching for you. I believed to my soul I would never see you again."

"But here I am," she said, needing to lighten the mood.

He smiled at that. "Yeah. And I'm so fucking thankful you are. Despite the circumstances."

She didn't want to get into the reminder of her father and the threat hanging over her. "What happened next?" she asked.

He lifted one tanned shoulder and her mouth watered. She wanted to press her lips to his skin but this conversation was so much more important and she needed to hear it all.

"Nothing. I worked, I graduated, and the deal Remy and I made let me buy The Back Door in Manhattan and open the P.I. agency."

"Why the P.I. agency?" she asked, knowing that without his skills for finding people and his help apprehending the senator's wife making him national news, she'd never have come to him for help. They'd never have this time together.

"Because it satisfies the adrenaline rush I used to

get from hacking into places and thinking the next click would lead me to you. And the first time I located someone, it was as a favor. I discovered finding missing people was damned fulfilling, so I got my P.I. license."

She reached for his hand. "It's fulfilling because of your mom. Because once her depression became too much for her to bear, she walked out and no one found her. No one helped her."

"To this day, you always knew me best." He reached for her, pulling her on top of him and she went willingly.

After all, she deserved one good thing in her life and Zach Dare had always been it.

SEX WITH HADLEY had exceeded Zach's expectations and he wanted nothing more than to stay in bed with her all day. Unfortunately, it was mid-morning and his day job beckoned. Which didn't mean he couldn't plan for tonight. While Hadley showered, he picked up the phone and put his idea in motion.

For his surprise to work, he needed Hadley out of the house so she wouldn't notice anything unusual. He'd decided to enjoy whatever time they had and if after, she still decided to leave, he'd have no choice but to let her go.

He needed to meet Remy and do paperwork. Knowing she had to tutor Maddox's brother later, she agreed to go with him in the early afternoon, but she asked him to give her something productive to do.

Once at the bar, he set her up with Sheila, who he knew would keep Hadley busy. After giving her a kiss on the cheek, he walked to his office and settled behind his desk. A couple of hours passed while he sorted through the bills, both paper and online emails, but he was unable to focus. Not when he couldn't stop reliving the night that should have happened years ago.

Yet, even he had to wonder, had they stayed together as teenagers, would they have lasted? He and Hadley were two very different people today, both shaped by a shared, painful past. One that had burned him so deeply, he hadn't let any woman in since.

So why was he holding on to hope now that he could convince Hadley to stay?

"Knock knock," Remy said from the doorway to the office.

"Come in. Want something to drink? I have my stash of Dirty Dare Tequila." He opened the bottom desk drawer and pulled out... an almost empty bottle. "What the fuck?"

Remy blinked. "Have you been indulging when no one's around? Or did you forget how much was left the last time?"

"Neither," Zach said through clenched teeth. "I haven't taken this out in a while. Between the missing bottles in our stock room and this, someone's brazen as hell."

Remy ran a hand over his bearded scruff. "Any ideas who's stealing?"

"Not a one. At this point, I don't trust anyone but you. I'm even wary of Maddox." Though he doubted his manager would betray them.

Lowering himself into the seat across from the desk, Remy leaned back and groaned. "You don't really think Maddox is drinking on the job or stealing, do you? The guy worked on Wall Street and his work ethic is admirable."

"I agree. But we need to know for certain and catch the SOB in the act. Whoever it is," Zach said, placing the bottle back in the drawer.

Though Remy nodded, he still didn't look happy, his mouth pulled into a tight line. "We already ran a background check on Maddox," he finally muttered. "The guy's clean and hasn't given us a day's worth of trouble. No issues except his brother..." Remy trailed off, the word lingering between them.

Zach agreed about Maddox, but when he met his partner's gaze, Remy's thoughts were clear. "Shit. You think it's Joe? That'll kill Maddox. He's been trying to get the kid on the straight and narrow."

Remy shrugged. "Only one way to find out."

"It's time to install cameras," Zach muttered. He didn't know why he hadn't done it sooner. Something about the laid-back atmosphere all year round had him become lax with security.

"I'm going to text Alpha Security and get the install set up asap. A day late and a dollar short," he muttered.

"Tell them to do the work after hours," Remy said. "I don't care what it costs. No need to give anyone a heads up that we're watching."

With a nod, Zach lifted his phone from the desk and shot off a text, giving Alpha his instructions. Thinking back on Joe, Zach knew it wasn't unusual for a teenager to lift bottles of liquor from their parents. No doubt, the kid thought of the bar the same way, what with Maddox being the manager. But Zach hoped they were wrong.

"Want me to ask Cal to bring us drinks?" he asked Remy, his hand still on his phone.

Remy shook his head. "It's fine. Let's move on to the next order of business."

"And what would that be?" Pushing back his chair, Zach stretched his legs out in front of him.

"How are things going with your ex?"

Zach raised an eyebrow. "Just come out and ask

me what you really want to know."

"Did you forgive her yet?" Remy asked.

"What do you think?" Zach didn't wait for an answer. "I was forced to look at the facts. She was sixteen. A good girl. A rule follower. The FBI said don't contact a soul or you'll put your entire family at risk so she did as she was told."

Zach wished he had that drink now. "Hadley also wanted to protect me from the Mob." Thinking he couldn't handle himself still rankled but at seventeen, she had a point. "It still grates on me but I understand, and don't hold it against her anymore. Her dirtbag father is another story."

Remy nodded. "What about getting in touch later on? After college? When the threat had passed? Something." Remy held up both hands before Zach could yell at him for not letting things go. "Come on, man. I'm on your side but I have to ask."

Forcing himself to relax his muscles and uncurl his fists, Zach nodded. He'd ask the same questions if the situation were reversed. "She said if she was going to have any kind of life, she had to make the best of her new reality and move on."

"And did she? Have any relationships?"

Zach's blood pressure rose. "We haven't gotten into specifics yet, but she's spent years working and raising her sister. I didn't get the impression she had much time for socializing," he muttered.

Hadley wasn't a virgin and despite what he'd said last night, it hurt to know she'd been with other men. She was right. He *should* have been her first.

Like everything else, he had to accept it and move on.

Chapter Twelve

HADLEY PLACED THE utensils in napkins and filled condiment bottles, happy to help Sheila, the hostess, get the front restaurant ready for the night's business. Since the tasks were mindless, she spent most of her time reliving last night with Zach, trying not to pine away for the years they'd missed. Appreciating the here and now was the smart move, so that's what she did.

Joe arrived late, sauntering in without a word of apology. Maddox, however, was aware of the time and walked over as his brother sat down, the teen grumbling under his breath. Hadley waited through the well-deserved lecture Maddox gave his sibling. When he finished, Maddox apologized to Hadley and forced his brother to do the same.

With their delayed start, by the time she finished working with Joe, it was after five p.m. "That's it for today," she said.

"Yes!" he shot his fist in the air.

She glanced at the teen, his longish brown hair falling over his eyes. "Be on time tomorrow," she told him firmly. "You've got this, Joe. You just need to do the reading each night and study. Show up and we'll go over themes and other pertinent information for your test."

"Not only will he study but he'll be here five minutes early." Maddox came up behind his brother and put a hand on his shoulder. "I'll be home each night and make sure of it. Right, Joe?"

"Yeah, yeah. Thanks, Ms. Stevens."

She smiled. Regardless of Joe's feelings towards school and studying, he'd obviously been taught manners. "You're very welcome."

"I'm thirsty. Soda?" Joe asked.

Maddox nodded. "Ask Cal. He's behind the bar."

Joe scrambled to his feet and rushed away, pulling his cell out as he ran.

"Thank you," Maddox said, running his hand through his hair in obvious frustration. "My parents sent him to me to keep him out of trouble and I've managed that much, barely. He just needs to pass his classes."

Hadley rose to her feet. "He will. Have faith."

"Hads!"

She turned at the sound of her sister's voice. Dani, Layla, and Zach's parents walked towards her.

"Hey!" She'd been texting with her sister and knew Dani was happy staying with the Dares but it was so good to see her.

"Hi," Michael said. "How's it going?"

"Quiet." Hadley didn't know if that was good or bad. She hadn't heard back from her father since she'd left a message using the burner phone he'd given her the day she'd arrived.

Though she was antsy, she knew Zach was watching out for her and digging into her father's background.

Michael nodded in understanding. "Where is Zach?"

"In his office with Remy."

"I'll go say hello." He left the women to talk and headed back.

Aware Dani was not going to accept a big hug in public, Hadley wrapped one arm loosely around her shoulder. "You look great." And wearing what had to be Layla's fringed denim shorts and cropped top. Teenagers, Hadley thought, suppressing a grin.

"We sat out by the pool today and tanned." Dani gestured towards her sunburned belly.

"I hope you wore sunscreen." The words came out automatically as did her sister's eyeroll.

Serenity chuckled. "They did. Girls, go ask for sodas," she said, and they too happily bounced off towards the bar. Serenity met her gaze. "Michael and I thought you'd want to see your sister in person."

Hadley gave her a grateful smile. "I appreciate it.

Being apart hasn't been easy. I'm so used to living under the same roof."

"It seems like you're the one raising her," Serenity said. "And doing a wonderful job. She's a lovely girl."

"And very outspoken," Hadley mused. "Seriously though, her mother isn't fit to do the job and obviously neither is our father. I decided not to move out and to be the adult and parent in the house. I don't regret my choice, either. I love her."

"I know you do." Serenity's soft gaze had always made Hadley feel warm and welcomed. "She's remarkably resilient."

Hadley nodded. A little too hardened for her age thanks to her mother's attitude and behavior but at heart, Dani was a good person.

The girls returned giggling and loudly whispering to each other. "He's so cute," Dani said to Layla, so engrossed in conversation, neither was aware anyone was paying attention to them.

"Older and hot." Layla waved a hand in front of her eyes. "He showed up at school after Christmas. He's living with his brother, the manager here."

Hadley felt her eyes open wide and land on Serenity's. Her thirteen-year-old sister was noticing Joe, a seventeen-year-old? She and Zach had been two years apart, but this was a four-year span.

Serenity put a hand on Hadley's shoulder and

shook her head, which Hadley took to mean, don't worry. Still oblivious to the adult attention, the girls made their way to a table and sat down.

"Layla's friends are her age," Serenity said, continuing to reassure Hadley. "They might be noticing Joe but there is no way he'll look twice at either one. They're too young but regardless, I promise to keep an eye on them."

Relieved, Hadley blew out a long breath. "Thank you. I am not ready for the boy-crazy stage." Not when she was deep in memories of her own teenage years and the love she'd had for her then-boyfriend.

"Hi, Mom."

As if Hadley's thoughts had conjured him, Zach strode over, his father by his side. He gave Serenity a kiss on the cheek.

"Hello, Zach," Serenity murmured.

He braced a hand on the back of the nearest chair. "What are you two deep in conversation about?"

Hadley shook her head, not wanting to get into her raising Dani now.

"We were just catching up," Serenity said.

"Where's Remy?" Hadley asked.

Zach pointed toward the back. "Still in the office but he'll head to his house in a little while."

Michael cleared his throat. "Hon, do you want to eat dinner here?"

Serenity nodded, a pleased smile on her face. "No cooking for me? Definitely. Let's go join the girls." She tilted her head towards the table where the kids sat.

Before Zach's parents could head over, the two teens jumped out of their seats and joined the group, both rambling at the same time.

Hadley caught the words *music festival*, *beach*, and *tonight*. Sheila had mentioned the concert on the beach to her earlier and warned Hadley people would start to line up to get boxed meals they'd preordered.

"Can we, Mom please?" Layla asked, bringing her palms together and begging with her gesture and voice.

Dani looked at Hadley with pleading eyes. "I never get to do something that fun at home. Can I go? Please?"

Hadley was at a loss because she knew nothing about safety at night in East Hampton, and the girls were staying with Serenity and Michael. The decision should be theirs. Hadley glanced at Zach, silently asking him what to say.

Zach folded his strong, muscled arms across his chest. "I think it would be fun if we all went," he said, those sexy lips she'd missed all day turning up in a grin.

The girls groaned, obviously upset the adults would ruin their fun.

Michael glanced at the teens. "Don't get all bent out of shape. We won't hang out with you, we'll just be in the area. Where we can keep an eye out." He raised an eyebrow, his stern expression letting them know the grownups would attend or the girls wouldn't go either.

"Fine," Layla said. "But don't embarrass me!"

"Ouch!" Michael playfully placed a hand over his heart.

Serenity laughed. "Let's get dinner, everyone. Do you two want to join us?" she looked to Zach, then Hadley.

He shook his head. "No, thanks. We have plans."

"We do?" she asked. Nothing had been mentioned earlier.

Zach slid his hand into hers, his palm warm as his fingers curled around hand. "Maddox," he called out, raising his voice so the manager would hear.

"Yeah, boss?"

"Did you ask Cal to handle things when you leave early?"

Hadley knew he wanted to be home with Joe until his test day. She glanced over in time to see Maddox give Zach a thumbs up.

"Great. We're out of here." They said goodbye to the Dares and their sisters, and Hadley let Zach lead her to his surprise.

★ ★ ★

ZACH LEFT REMY taking a call in his office and stopped by the kitchen to make sure everything was running smoothly. With the concert tonight, the bar would be packed with takeout pickups. But nobody's meal would come close to what he had planned.

He joined his family and once they'd agreed to be at the festival later, he grasped Hadley's hand and led her to his car. Before he opened her door, his gaze lingered on her. Though he'd seen Hadley this morning, now he took his time, slowly taking her in. She was so pretty in an understated way.

He doubted she was even aware of how hot she looked in a pink, yellow and white, floral mini dress. The ruffled V-neck collar exposed a delicate hint of cleavage and the flirty hem fluttered mid-thigh. Her tanned legs enticed him and he wanted to feel those long limbs wrapped around his waist as he thrusted deep.

But that would happen later. Right now, he had other plans.

He pulled open the car door. "Hop in," he said.

"Where are we going?" she asked, as she lifted herself into the SUV.

He grinned. "Patience, grasshopper."

She rolled her eyes. "You always did like *The Karate*

Kid."

"And some things don't change." Like how he felt about her. He strode around the vehicle and settled into the driver's seat, turning on the motor.

"Give me a hint?" He glanced over.

She'd pursed her lips, and it was either kiss her senseless or appease her curiosity. If he put his lips on hers, they'd never leave. "We're going to eat in a secluded spot where we can hear the band, and after we have some alone time, we'll go help my parents with the girls."

"Like a picnic?" she asked, hopefully.

He nodded. "Just like it." On a grander scale.

"I'd love that!" Happiness flickered in her eyes, her dark lashes fringing the light blue orbs. "And thank you. I'm sure the last thing you want to do is hang around with crowds of people but…"

"You want to keep an eye on Dani. I get it." Though he was certain his parents could handle things without them, he knew Hadley would feel better if she could watch her sister.

"Smart man." She leaned over and kissed his cheek, his skin tingling where she'd touched. "And I appreciate it."

He put the car in drive and he headed out, returning to his house. Once they were out of the car, he grasped her hand again and led her through his locked gate. They strode around the grounds and into the back, passing the pool and continuing down to the water.

By the time they walked down the stairs to the dock and beach, her mouth was open as she watched the waves come in, the sun still high in the blue, cloud-dusted sky.

"You have this view every day of the summer?" she asked in awe, her voice breathless. "It's gorgeous."

He turned, catching her profile. No, *she* was gorgeous. "Believe me, I know how fortunate I am." And he wasn't talking about the horizon.

"Come on. This way." He turned right and soon his surprise came into view. He'd called his sister, Jade, who ran parties at their family hotel in Manhattan, and she'd come up with the name of a Hamptons party planner who specialized in small, intimate gatherings, including a party of two.

Money and connections talked and he'd convinced the owner to handle an elaborate same day picnic. At a glance, the woman had outdone herself. An oversized blanket… no, it looked more like a cream-colored rug that wouldn't have divots thanks to the sand, had been spread out on the beach.

Floral bundles in a variety of pinks lined one blanket edge. Two formal place settings, complete with linen light pink napkins, waited for them along with a champagne bucket, complete with a bottle being chilled in ice. Lanterns lined two other sides of the blanket for when the sun set, and citronella candles would protect them from bugs.

He turned from the spread to Hadley, who stared with wide eyes. "Hads?" He liked her sister's nickname for her and unless she asked him not to use it, he decided it was time to adopt it, too.

She pivoted to face him, her eyes glassy with tears. "I'm… speechless."

"But do you like it?" he asked, suddenly worried it was too much. His family's financial status had always put her off and she'd been keeping a tally of what he'd spent on her and Dani since she'd arrived.

"I do. So much."

He nodded. "Good." Honesty was the only way to go and if he gave her something to consider over the next days or weeks, then he'd accomplished more than the goal of making her happy.

"Why did you go to all this effort?" she asked.

He cleared his throat, his own emotions too close to the surface as he raised one shoulder in a half-shrug. "I don't know how much time we have together, and I want to make the most of it."

She stepped closer, wrapped her arms around his neck and sealed her lips against his. With a groan, he hooked one arm around her waist and pulled her against him, loving every second of the way she set the pace. Slow and steady, she licked his bottom lip, drawing a moan from deep in his chest and when he parted his mouth, she slid her tongue inside.

The emotional kiss seemed to last forever and when she pulled back, her lips glistening as much as her eyes, he was overcome, too.

"Let's go eat," he said gruffly.

They sat side by side on pillows and enjoyed. He finger-fed her egg and tuna salad bite-sized sandwiches, they drank champagne from glass flutes, and for dessert, they dipped fresh strawberries in melted chocolate. All the while, they talked about life.

"You can hear the band music from here?" she asked, licking the chocolate off her fingers.

Somehow he suppressed a groan. "You sure can. But I have a special spot for that, too."

A few minutes of silence lingered and she seemed to be gearing up to say something. "What's going on, Hads?"

"I called my father earlier today. He didn't pick up. Again."

He grasped her hand. "We're working on it." He hadn't been keeping her in the loop as they found information because he wanted to wait until he had a full picture.

But she seemed to need something now. "So far

Remy's linked him to certain associates and let's just say they're more deeply Mob connected than I imagined."

She shook her head. "I know what you mean. I was hoping he'd learned something from having to run the first time but obviously not. I knew as much when that guy cornered me by my car."

She shuddered and Zach pulled her against him with one arm. "You're safe here."

"As soon as I saw your face in that magazine, I knew you were the only choice." She drew up straighter and he released her. "Now, can we talk about something else?"

She obviously wanted to forget so he asked her questions about school, teaching, her students, and friends, topics meant to keep the conversation light.

"Tell me about your siblings. What do they do for a living? I assume they all have the same work ethic you do."

He nodded. "Nick runs the hotels, Jade is the Event Coordinator, Asher founded Dirty Dare Vodka which later became Dirty Dare Spirts as he expanded. He insisted we all invest, and the business took off. And of course, you know about Harrison, the famous actor and producer." He grinned, proud of them all. "Then there are my half-siblings. You know Layla and the triplets are away at college."

She shook her head, smiling. "I don't know how Serenity and Michael corralled you all."

"I have no clue." He just knew they were one big, happy family.

"I met Jade and Nick's girls," Hadley said of his nieces. "What about Harrison and Asher? Any kids?"

He leaned back on his hands. "Harrison and Winter have a girl, Jules, named after her late mother, Julianna. As for Asher, he and Nikki aren't ready yet. She's much younger and they wanted to wait."

She pulled her knees up, wrapping her arms around them. "So all the Dare men have baby girls. I love it. I can imagine each with a shotgun in hand when they're old enough date." Hadley's grin was infectious, and he laughed.

"You are so right."

She glanced his way. "Someone's due for a boy."

A little boy with Hadley's silky brown hair with streaks of blonde and her light blue eyes, flashed through his mind. The possibility warmed him, filling empty spaces inside him he hadn't paid attention to before. Except that was a dream that wouldn't be coming true. She hadn't said or done anything to indicate her plans had changed.

"Which siblings are you closest to?" she asked.

"All of them." Thanks to his contacts and *skills*, Zach was the brother everyone turned to in times of crisis and he was grateful he could help. Family meant everything to him, something his biological mother's illness and suicide had reinforced.

"I really envy you that," she murmured.

He wanted to tell her she could have that too. His family could be hers. Something that couldn't happen if she went home. But he remained silent. Convincing her by showing her what they could have was one thing. Verbally pushing her was another. She needed to come to her decision to stay or go on her own.

The rest of his meal went down like sawdust until he told himself he had time to show her everything they could share after her father's issues ended.

If she agreed to stay.

Once they finished eating, he stood, pulling her to her feet.

"Shouldn't we clean up?" she asked.

He shook his head. "Tonight is for you to enjoy." The service included set up, décor, food and cleanup later.

He clasped her hand and led her to another blanket a little farther down the beach. There were backrests set up along with lanterns and citronella torches burning behind them.

They settled in, resting beside each other, the conversation still flowing and when pauses happened, they were comfortable and easy, the silence peaceful. This was what he'd never had with another woman. What he'd watched his siblings find and what Zach both needed and had been missing.

Because *Hadley* had been missing.

Music sounded in the distance, the band tuning up. He resettled them against the cushions and pulled her into his arms.

Chapter Thirteen

When Hadley fled her home, she expected to be alone with her sister and afraid for their lives. Instead she was wrapped in the arms of the man she'd always loved and her sister was with people she trusted. Her father was in the wind but there wasn't anything she could do about that. So she intended to enjoy the evening with Zach and face one day at a time. It was all she could do. Because her life wasn't here.

After she'd arrived in the Hamptons, she'd called school and explained she'd had a family emergency and had to rush out of town without notice. Principal Doyle had been understanding. He'd wished her the best and said he'd see her at the end of the summer. Which was the issue.

Would her situation be resolved by then? She needed to go back or risk losing tenure and her student loan coverage. She couldn't afford to start over as a first-year teacher with a first-year salary, nor could she take the financial hit of losing her student loan forgiveness. Not to mention that her sister needed her life, her friends and stability.

"Where'd you go?" Zach's deep voice brought her back to the present.

She shook her head in a futile attempt to push the future out of her thoughts. "Sorry. Just thinking."

He kissed her forehead. "Well don't. The music is too good not to let it take you away."

"You're right." The strains of the music calmed her and she snuggled closer.

Zach placed a hand high up on her thigh and her skin immediately began to tingle. He didn't rush, just leisurely brushed his thumb back and forth. Resting her head on his shoulder, she closed her eyes, only to realize he was slowly moving his hand. He inched upward until that same finger traced the line along the crease of her thigh.

Her body responded, her panties growing wet with desire and a throbbing need pulsed in her sex. She arched her pelvis and began to roll her hips in circles, silently begging him to relieve the ache he was causing.

A new band took over and the music turned to country, the beat more in time to the throbbing of her clit. She moaned and he reacted, sliding his fingers beneath her string-bikini underwear, gliding over her slick sex. His fingers skated over her outer lips, squeezing them together, teasing her, touching her everywhere except where she needed him the most.

"Are you ready for more?" he whispered in her

ear.

"So ready." She had no idea what he intended, nor did she care as long as she came.

He slid his arm out from behind her and slid downward. Grasping her panties, he yanked hard, ripping them off her thighs. She lifted her ass and he pulled, tossing the flimsy garment aside. Her pussy was bare to the warm night air and she didn't care. As much as being out in the open turned her on, she also knew this was private property and no one would see.

She spread her legs wide and he climbed between them, stretching his legs as he lay down. He dipped his head and his mouth covered her sex. She moaned as he began to devour her, his warm breath heating her outside and his tongue and teeth doing obscene things that had her trembling.

He thrust one finger into her, then another, pumping the long digits in and out while his tongue latched onto her clit and played. And God, he was talented. She never knew sex could be like this, so all-consuming and divine. As much as she needed to fly, she never wanted it to end.

He continued his sensual assault and finally, he curled his fingers inside her, his teeth grazed her clit, and she followed the waves of pleasure as they crashed over her.

She screamed not caring if her voice carried.

"Zach, yes. I'm coming, don't stop."

He didn't, continuing to pump his fingers and lick her sex until she was sated, her body nothing more than a limp noodle. He sat up, a pleased smile on his lips. Then, his gaze hot on hers, he licked those fingers clean.

As she lay back, her breathing ragged, he reached over, opened a cooler she hadn't noticed before, and grabbed a bottle of water. He unscrewed the top and handed her the bottle which she gratefully took and guzzled it down.

He drank the other half, replaced the cap and tossed the bottle next to the cooler. He slid back over to her, and she cupped her hand over the bulge in his jeans, the outline of his rigid cock impossible to miss. Incredibly, her pussy pulsed and she realized she could, in a few minutes, want him inside her.

But he grasped her wrist, halting the hand that was kneading him. "Tonight was all for you," he said in a gravelly voice. "Besides, we need to go check on the girls."

She raised her eyebrows. "And you're saying I can't convince you that a quickie would make it easier for you to get through the concert, the crowds, the teenagers?" As she asked, she flicked her fingers and unbuttoned his jeans.

Turns out, she didn't have to do any more convincing. And she discovered that sex on the beach was a beautiful thing. As long as she was with Zach.

TWO WEEKS LATER, Zach sat in his office, watching the video of the bar and office for the fifth time, hating that he and Remy had been right. The thief was Maddox's brother, Joe. The kid had laid low for a couple of weeks, no doubt aware he'd fucked up by drinking from Zach's personal stash.

He hadn't even been smart enough to pour water in to make it look full. Something he and his brothers had done as kids. Which was why he was more annoyed by the hassle he'd been put through than the action. Maddox would have to deal with his brother. Zach saw Joe last night sneaking past his brother, into the back, and slipping out the back door with a bottle.

For someone in the P.I. business, Zach had fucked up twice, not having installed cameras and not having a lock on the stock room door but it was damned hard to keep things secure during a busy night. Lesson learned. The only reason he hadn't installed a lock along with the cameras was so he could catch the thief in the act. He'd called Remy in the city, and they'd agreed on how to handle things.

A knock sounded on the door. "Come in."

Maddox stepped inside and he shut the door behind him. "What is it, boss? It sounded urgent."

Zach placed his cell on the desk and rose to his feet. "Have a seat."

"You're standing. I'll stand, too. Just lay it on me," Maddox said, now tense, arms folded defensively across his chest.

"I know who's stealing the alcohol."

The manager raised his eyebrows. "If you're about to accuse me—"

"No." Zach cut him off. "Not at all. But I do think you should sit down for this." To make his point, Zach walked around his desk and lowered himself into the seat, hoping to make the other man more comfortable.

Eyes narrowed, Maddox sat down across from him. "Who is it?"

Zach hated this shit. "Your brother. And I don't expect you to take my word for it, so… here." He lifted his phone off the desk, opened the saved section of the video and passed it to Maddox.

The man he'd entrusted his bar to tapped the screen and shook his head, his mouth pulled into a tight line. "Dammit." He slid the phone back to Zach.

Maddox lifted his gaze. "No need to fire me. I'll grab my shit and get out of here. I know you trusted me and I'm sorry. Send me a bill for the damages."

Bracing his hands on the arms of the chair, he pushed himself to his feet.

"Sit the fuck down," Zach muttered. "You're not going anywhere. Just because your brother screwed up and is acting like a teenager, that isn't on you."

Maddox shook his head. "I should have known but other than school, he hasn't been giving me as hard a time as he did my parents. I promised them I'd keep an eye on him." He rubbed his palms against his eyes. "Can I have the night off? My brother and I need to have a talk."

Zach nodded. "Of course. Quit blaming yourself. You know teenagers are notorious for getting into trouble. You'll figure out how to handle him."

Maddox raised an eyebrow.

"What?"

He leaned forward. "I just did. What would you say to him bussing tables here for the rest of the summer? For free." Maddox worked his jaw, his frustration obvious. "Unless… you plan on calling the police."

Zach paused, thinking about how to explain his and Remy's decision. "I considered it but… like I said. He's a kid. I'm not going to ruin the rest of his life because he thought he could pull one over on his older brother." He rose to his feet. "As for him working here—"

"I'll keep an eye on him and when I can't, I'll fill Cal in. Joe will never have access to the liquor again."

"Oh, I know. There's a lock on the storage door now and no bottles in my desk. And not only will the bar be manned twenty-four-seven, but the cameras send a live feed to my phone and to the security company. Let Joe know we're watching him. And if it happens again, we will call the police."

Maddox nodded. "I will."

"And if bussing tables is how you want to handle things, it's fine. Just scare the shit out of him first."

Maddox stood and approached him, holding out a hand that Zach shook. "Thank you. I appreciate you not giving the kid a record for the rest of his life. Mind if I ask why?"

Zach shook his head and grinned. "Someone cut me a break one day and I'm just repaying the favor." Even if the person who helped him was a fed.

"And now I need to get home."

"She seems like a great woman," Maddox said. He was obviously referring to Hadley.

"Yeah. She is."

"Is she sticking around?"

Since Maddox had no idea about Hadley's situation, and Zach had no intention of betraying her by discussing it with an outsider, he merely shook his head. "Last I heard, that's not her plan."

★　★　★

HADLEY HAD SETTLED into a routine with Zach. She'd moved into his bedroom and they were sharing a bed, something that felt as natural as breathing. She'd wake up to him sliding inside her and immediately forced her mind to enjoy what they shared for as long as possible and block out everything that worried her. And there was a lot.

Not hearing back from her father had her freaked out. Even Dani had begun to ask why she couldn't talk to her dad, and her sister's questions along with his silence had Hadley spiraling. Zach had spoken to some of his old FBI contacts but they claimed to know nothing about Gregg Stevens or Hank Roberts, as her dad was originally known.

Most days, Zach went to the bar around midday. Hadley would meet him there around three and help Sheila set up for the evening. She became someone who jumped in wherever she was needed and instead of being paid under the table, which wasn't comfortable for her, she agreed to let Zach help when she needed it. The compromise worked for her and she felt like she was earning her way.

Today, she'd called and let him know she wasn't coming in to work because she had a headache. In truth, she wanted to make him a special, surprise dinner to thank him for all he'd done for her and her sister. Before she needed to figure out how to get him home earlier than usual, as they usually stayed at the bar, he insisted he was coming home to check on her after the dinner rush.

Now, she stood in his state-of-the-art kitchen, drinking a glass of pinot noir, while her dinner simmered. Since she'd arrived, she'd been dying to put the kitchen to good use but they'd rarely been home at dinner time. After today, she was in love with the space. Though she doubted Zach cooked much, the appliances were new and a chef's dream. Not that she was a professional but the tiny kitchen back home with little counter space made cooking anything difficult.

A beep sounded, the warning on the doors thanks to the alarm system, letting her know Zach had walked in from the garage.

She drew a deep breath and waited for him to join her.

"Hey." Zach strode into the room, looking as good as when he'd left this morning. The black T-shirt molded to his skin. Scruff from his five o'clock shadow covered his cheeks. And she had the light scratches on her thighs to remind her how good his face felt between her legs.

He was so sexy he took her breath away. "Hi, yourself," she murmured.

"You don't look like you have a headache," he said, his gaze devouring her, making her glad she'd chosen the curve-hugging dress.

"That's because I don't. I wanted to surprise you with dinner." Smiling, she picked up an extra glass of wine and walked towards him. "I know you aren't a wine person but it goes well with the meal I cooked."

He accepted the glass, his gaze warm on hers. "You didn't have to cook for me."

"I know. But I wanted to. Call it a thank you for everything."

He shook his head and sighed. "It smells delicious. I just don't want you feeling obligated to me in any way."

"Good because I don't. Are your ready to eat now or we can wait?"

"I'll go wash up and be right back." He placed the wine on the counter and brushed his lips over hers.

As always, she sank into him, enjoying and absorbing every moment for her memory banks.

He lifted his head and started for the hall.

"Oh!" she exclaimed.

He turned.

"Are you going back to the bar tonight?" She wanted to know if this was a leisurely dinner or if she needed to keep things moving through dessert.

He shook his head. "Rough night. I had to tell

Maddox I caught his brother on camera stealing alcohol."

"Joe? Oh no!" She shook her head. "He's definitely going through some rough teenage angst," she said. "I hope Maddox can get through to him. How did he take it?"

Zach shrugged. "Not badly? I think Joe was doing worse when he was living at his parents'. Maybe it wasn't such a huge shock to Maddox. But he asked if he could put the kid to work bussing tables for free and I agreed."

She couldn't help but smile. "That was kind of you."

"I would have stayed home regardless if you weren't well but now that I know you're fine..." His gaze raked over her, approval in his heated stare. "The Back Door II can definitely run without me."

His words warmed her. She'd been hoping for a long, leisurely night, just the two of them. "Good. But I am curious. How in the world did you come up with that name? Because it can't be after the Urban Dictionary definition."

An adorable smirk lifted his lips. "You're a dirty girl, aren't you?"

She blushed and shook her head. "Cut that out."

He chuckled. "The name has two meanings, at least for me. The main entrance in the city bar is through the back door, and it's also a nod to my hacking skills." He winked at her and strode out the door, leaving her smiling.

ZACH SAT BESIDE Hadley at the kitchen table he rarely used. When he was here alone, he stood as he ate or sat at the bar stools by the counter. He enjoyed coming home to Hadley. Even more, he liked the routine they'd fallen into. It was the way things were always meant to be. Or more like a tease, showing him what he could have had, but was going to lose when her SOB father finally surfaced, and they figured out how to make sure the girls were safe. Then Hadley would be leaving again.

He shook his head, refusing to think about that now. "Incredible dinner." She'd served them bacon-wrapped, honey-glazed pork, garlic-steamed broccoli, and now they were finishing slices of a chocolate cake she'd picked up in town.

She beamed at the compliment. "Thank you. I don't get to do much gourmet cooking at home. Tiny kitchen, no counter space."

He watched as she licked the fork, her tongue cleaning each of the tines and he wanted those strokes on his cock next. It was hard and aching inside his jeans.

Letting out a low groan of need, he braced his hands on the table to push out his chair when the doorbell rang.

"Who could that be?" Hadley asked.

"I'll go check and get rid of them," he said, annoyed the effort she had gone to was being interrupted.

He strode out of the kitchen and walked to the front door, swinging it open. "What the hell do you want–Mom? Dad? What are you doing here?" He stepped aside so they could enter, shutting the door behind them.

Serenity's eyes were red-rimmed and Zach's senses went on alert.

"Is there any chance Dani and Layla are here?" his dad asked.

"No… why?"

His mom wrung her hands "The girls snuck out and neither are answering their phones."

"What?" He turned to see Hadley grasping onto the nearest doorframe for support.

His father held up a hand. "It could be teenage stupidity but—"

"It could be related to my father. Oh my God." Hadley put her hand over her mouth, her face losing color.

"I'm so sorry." Serenity shook her head.

"I don't blame you for anything." Hadley walked up to her. "You've done more than I could have hoped for when I showed up at the bar. I'm scared but I'm not at all upset with you."

His mom blew out a long breath of air. "Thank you for that."

"What happened, exactly?" Zach asked.

"The girls asked if they could have a late dinner in town with friends, and Layla said Jenny's mom would drive them home. Once the girls were thirty minutes late, I called to check on them. Layla texted back and said, *home soon*. When they didn't show up and stopped answering their phones, I called Jenny's mother but she said Jenny had been home all night."

"So Layla lied." Michael put his hand around Serenity's waist and eased her into him.

"And maybe they're just pulling teenage shit," Zach said, hoping to calm Hadley down.

"I want to call my sister." She turned and ran for the kitchen, Zach rushing after her, his parents following behind.

Hadley's hands trembled as she picked up her phone from the counter and touched the screen. "Come on, come on, pick up."

Too much time passed and finally she disconnected the call and shook her head. "No answer." She paced the length of the kitchen. "I knew it's been too quiet," she mumbled to herself. "I should never have put your family in the middle." She twisted her hands as she looked past him. "I'm sorry."

"There's no reason for you to be sorry, either," Serenity said. "We just need to find them."

Ignoring the fact that his parents were in the room, Zach caught Hadley's hand and pulled her to him. "Hey. Look at me."

She met his gaze, her eyes wide and filled with fear.

"I understand why you're panicking but we don't know anything yet. The fact that they obviously lied to stay out later than curfew is a good sign as far as it not being related to your dad."

Hadley nodded but her shoulders were hunched down and she'd withdrawn into herself. Not that he blamed her. With all the shit her father was into, there was always a reason to worry.

"The good news is, when I bought Dani's phone, I brought it home and set it up so I could track her." He pulled his cell from his pocket and pulled up the information. "Dani's phone shows her moving down your street as we speak." He glanced at his parents, then lifted Hadley's chin. "Hear that? The girls are on their way home."

Her body shuddered, the action working to shake off her panicked mood. "When I get my hands on my sister, I am going to kill her."

Zach met his parents' gaze. "Looks like we're heading back to your house."

Serenity nodded in agreement. She glanced around the kitchen, her eyes widening as she took in the kitchen for the first time. "We interrupted your dinner."

Hadley let out a laugh that sounded sweet to Zach's ears. "Another reason to throttle them."

"Come on. We have teenagers to lecture," Zach said. As his parents turned and walked out of the room, he pulled Hadley close. "When we get home, we will pick this up. In bed."

She wrapped her arms around him and buried her face in his neck. "Thank you," she whispered.

He inhaled her sexy, arousing scent, his cock growing hard. "You're welcome," he told her. And then he reminded his dick that satisfaction would have to wait.

Chapter Fourteen

HADLEY AND ZACH followed his parents to their house. He left her to her thoughts, giving her anger time to grow. "How could Dani be so selfish?" she asked as they pulled into the driveaway. "She knows I'd worry!"

Zach placed his hand on her leg and squeezed. "She's a teenager and they only think about their wants and needs. Trust me, between Layla and the triplets, I've seen it all."

"Yeah, I guess."

He cut the engine and turned to her. "Stay calm. She won't hear you if you're yelling."

They stepped out of the car and she rushed up the walk.

"Layla Dare, you get yourself in front of me right now! I've been worried sick!"

"Sounds like we don't have to worry about you yelling, Serenity is doing it for you."

They ran inside and stopped short as the girls came to greet them. Layla's eyes were red as was the tip of her nose. Her makeup was smeared and she had tear streaks on her face. Dani stepped beside her, her head down, as if she couldn't meet anyone's gaze.

"Divide and conquer," Michael said. "Layla, let's go to your room. Dani, take your sister to the family room."

Given Michael's strict tone of voice, Layla dragged herself back the way she'd come and her parents followed.

"Dani?" Hadley asked.

"This way." She led them to a large room with an oversized sofa and club chairs and plopped down into a chair.

Zach pulled Hadley towards the couch and she lowered herself into an unbelievably soft cushion, Zach beside her.

"Well? Where were you tonight?" Hadley asked, her heart still racing even though her sister was safe and in front of her.

Dani's pink hair fell over her face. "We went to a bonfire on the beach."

Hadley drew a deep breath and tried not to lose her temper. "Why was Layla crying? Because her parents are angry?"

"No." Dani tucked her hair behind one hear. "She has a crush on Maddox's brother. That's why we went. And he told her she was a kid and to go home."

Despite her frustration, Hadley winced. "That had to hurt. But it doesn't change the fact that you two missed curfew, lied about how you were getting home... how *did* you get home?"

"We took an Uber."

Hadley forced herself to take a deep breath, then another. Zach's hand came to rest on her back and she appreciated the support.

Leaning forward, she met her sister's gaze, her tone and expression serious. "Dani, I appreciate that you want to have fun but Michael and Serenity are doing us a favor by letting you stay here. I also get that you went along with Layla. I'm not pinning blame on her. But we're here for a reason and I've been giving you a lot of leeway because nobody knows where we are, and we've taken every precaution. But rules are rules. And not answering your phone and scaring the crap out of us is not okay. *Ever.*"

"I know. But—"

"No buts! What if someone had taken you?"

Tears filled Dani's eyes, her mouth quivering. "I'm sorry."

Hadley nodded. "Never again. Promise me."

"Promise." Dani rose and walked over. Hadley met her halfway and pulled her into a hug. "I want you to apologize to Zach's parents, too."

Hadley felt Dani nod into her shoulder. "If Layla is grounded in any way, so are you. Deal?"

Another nod. As Hadley knew from experience,

the only time Dani was quiet was when she knew she'd been wrong. Hadley was just grateful they were safe.

Once they talked to Serenity and Michael, who assured her there would be punishment, and Dani had apologized to her hosts, Hadley thanked them again and hugged her sister. Then Zach took her home.

ZACH WOKE UP before Hadley. First order of business was to make himself a cup of coffee. Last night had been stressful and exhausting and when they finally came home, Hadley had washed up, slipped into one of his old T-shirts, crawled into bed and fell fast asleep. She planned on cleaning the kitchen from the meal they'd walked out on this morning. Instead of waking her, he handled the mess himself.

He needed the time to think. Though he'd kept quiet last night, letting his parents handle Layla and Hadley deal with her sister, he knew Hadley had been petrified. He also knew he'd made an error. One he'd corrected. Before leaving, he'd asked the girls to unlock their phones and hand them over. Now he was tracking them both. If anything had happened to them because he'd screwed up, he'd never have forgiven himself.

Once he finished cleaning, he took his coffee and

walked outside to the back yard, settling into an upright lounge seat and stretching his legs in front of him. The weather was typically hot since it was almost July but the ocean breeze felt good.

He placed the mug on a side-table, closed his eyes and tilted his face toward the sun. If he didn't think about the past or the future, life was perfect. He had the woman of his dreams in his bed and a life he'd worked hard to achieve. But he couldn't ignore the facts. He needed to find Hadley's father and make sure the sisters were safe.

He picked up his phone and pulled up his list of numbers, dialing his partner.

"Morning. What's going on?" Remy said by way of greeting.

"Hey. I'm going to need you to take a trip to Illinois." He explained what had happened last night with his sister and Dani. "I don't want to risk that next time there really is something to worry about. You need to find out what happened to her father. I'd go but I don't want to leave Hadley here alone."

"You got it. I'll check in with our fed friends first. Andrews owes me a favor. If he can't find out anything more I'll head out," Remy said.

Zach breathed out a sigh of relief. "Thanks. I owe you one."

"Friends don't get markers. I'll be in touch. Say

hello to your girl."

"Yeah." If only she was his girl for good.

They said goodbye and Zach disconnected the call.

"Everything okay?" Hadley stood before him in jean shorts cut high around her thighs, his T-shirt tied in a knot around her waist, her hair pulled up in a messy bun and no makeup. She was comfortable with herself and that was as sexy as everything else about her.

She sat down on the chair beside him, a cup of coffee in her hand.

"I didn't hear you come outside. Yeah. Everything is fine." He wasn't going to keep anything from her. "I asked Remy to go to your hometown and see if he can find your dad and see what he's gotten himself into."

Her eyes opened wide. "Really? Thank you." She inhaled deeply and met his gaze. "I spent my entire life protecting Dani and I can't let anything happen to her now."

"Don't worry, sweetheart. I've been working on figuring out who your father's associates are since you showed up at the bar. I waited awhile before asking Remy to go because you left a hot situation and I wanted to give things a chance to settle."

She nodded. "Will Remy be okay?"

"He knows how to handle himself and get answers." Zach didn't mention the FBI friend. Whatever information they ultimately found, he'd share with her then.

"Oh! Thanks for cleaning the kitchen." She set her mug on the table, rose, stepped in front of him and crawled into his lap. "I don't know what I did to deserve you but I'm so grateful."

He held her close, burying his nose in her neck and rubbing up and down, inhaling her arousing floral scent.

"Are you sniffing me?" she asked, laughing.

He chuckled but it was no joke. "Whatever that scent is, it makes me fucking hard."

"Yes, it does," she murmured, rocking herself over his erection. "It's sweet pea body wash and shampoo. It's got pear, raspberry, some musk…"

"You. It smells like you." He groaned and licked her neck, causing her to tremble.

He wanted nothing more than to strip off her shorts and panties and bury himself deep inside her wet pussy. As he reached for the button at her waist, his cell rang on the table.

"Ignore it," he muttered, flicking open the button and pulling down her zipper.

The ringing stopped, thank God.

"Lift your hips."

She pushed herself up and he wriggled her shorts down her legs. And his phone began ringing again.

"Get it. It must be important," she said, re-settling herself in his lap but now he felt the wet heat of her panties.

He picked up the cell and glanced at the screen, seeing Raven's number, before answering the call on a growl. "It better be important if you aren't calling Remy."

"Sorry, boss. You're going to want to know. That car you told me to keep an eye on?"

Immediately on alert, he stiffened. "What about it?"

"It was impounded overnight."

"They fucking towed it?"

Hadley stiffened. "My car?" she whispered.

He nodded.

"Noo. I can't afford those fees." He squeezed her waist in reassurance.

"I know you told everyone not to report the car as illegally parked," Raven was saying. "But I went home sick and… well… I didn't think to let one of the guys who'd been on vacation know and he called the towing company. He said he was trying to help but he was just trying to kiss your ass since he left us short-handed for a week longer than planned. Sorry. If there's anything I can do…"

"Raven, chill. It's fine. Thanks for letting me know. Are you feeling better?" No matter how much of a hassle this happened to be for Hadley, he liked Raven and had been a dick when he'd answered her call.

"Yeah, thank you. Just one of those things." She didn't elaborate and he didn't ask. He wouldn't have made her manager if he didn't know she did a damn good job and only took off when necessary.

"Good. Favor?" he asked.

"Of course."

He shifted Hadley in his lap. Though he was on the phone, his dick was still half-hard and he wasn't comfortable. "Call Dario down at the impound lot. Ask him not to return the car and to park it somewhere locked up and safe. I'll pay the tow fee but remind him he owes me and not to charge the daily rate."

He winked at Hadley in an attempt to calm her down. If he'd had a view of her brain, he knew he'd see the ever-working calculator adding what she owed.

"You got it, boss. On it right now. Bye."

Zach disconnected the call and put the phone back on the table.

Hadley shook her head. "Seriously? I can not even afford the tow fee."

She'd been working her ass off at the bar in the evenings and though she'd finished tutoring Maddox's brother and he'd more than passed his test, word had gotten around. Hadley had a few more students she was tutoring during various times of the day, but she wasn't making much. And she couldn't access her bank account without alerting anyone to her location.

"Did I ask you to pay?"

She sighed and he understood her feelings.

With her meager earnings, she already insisted on paying for groceries, and even if he used his credit card, she'd stuff cash in places for him to find. He'd given up trying to return her money and was keeping an envelope to give back before she went home.

Not something he wanted to think about now.

Knowing the mood for sex had been broken he tapped her thigh. "Did you eat breakfast?"

She shook her head.

"Let's go into town and get something to eat, okay?"

"But—"

He leaned in and kissed her, shutting up any argument she might want to have.

JULY 4th BROUGHT the entire Dare family to the Hamptons to celebrate Independence Day and enjoy the long weekend. Dani fit in like she belonged. With a hot dog in one hand and a red solo cup filled with soda in the other, she sat with Layla and the triplets on a blanket at the far end of the backyard lawn, waiting for the fireworks to begin. The boys looked like a combination of their parents and Hadley would be lucky if Dani didn't end up crushing on one or all three college boys.

The adults had settled nearby, their babies asleep inside with Mrs. Baker, their shared housekeeper. Since Hadley had already spent time with Jade and Knox, Aurora and Nick, and Michael and Serenity, she and Zach sat on a blanket by Asher, the oldest sibling and his twenty-two-year-old wife, Nikki. Next to them were Harrison and Winter, Nikki's half-sister.

"So, Hadley, how does it feel to be back?" Nikki asked.

She was a pretty woman with olive skin, her long, dark hair pulled up in a messy bun. She once modeled, something Hadley could see since even without makeup, Nikki was delicate looking and beautiful.

She was also sweet to her husband's more grumpy nature.

Since there was a five-year age difference between Asher and Zach, Hadley hadn't known him as well as the other siblings. But she felt his glare now and wondered if he held her disappearance against her because she'd hurt his brother.

Still, Nikki was making an effort to get to know Hadley, and she liked the younger woman. "It feels…

good." Better than good, she thought, leaning against Zach's strong chest.

"After a few bumps in the road by way of explaining where you've been for the last oh, ten years," Asher said, his tone snide as he didn't bother to hide his cynicism.

His narrowed gaze gave Hadley the chills and she stiffened.

"Asher!" Nikki nudged her husband in the side. "Be nice. Zach and Hadley's relationship is none of your business. They're obviously happy now and we should be pleased for them."

"Agreed," Zach said, his body taut, his muscles vibrating with anger. "And if you can't be nice, Asher, go take another blanket to watch the fireworks. One far away from here." He wrapped his arms around Hadley protectively.

"It's fine," she said, not wanting to cause a fight between them. Especially when Asher had fair points. "Your brother's reaction is understandable." She'd hurt his sibling and Asher Dare wasn't the most easy going of the brothers.

"It's not, because he knows why you disappeared and that it wasn't your fault."

"Remember how you jumped to conclusions and misjudged me before you even knew me?" Nikki placed her fingers beneath her husband's chin and turned him to face her. "You told me you learned from your mistakes. Are you saying I can't trust your word?"

"Of course you can," he said, leaning forward and kissing her, his lips lingering as if no one else were around.

Unable to control herself, Hadley laughed.

"What?" Asher bit out.

She grinned. "I just like how your wife handles you."

Both Nikki and Zach chuckled at her comment.

"Hadley's got a point," Nikki said.

"So... truce?" Hadley met Asher's gaze and extended her hand.

Nikki nudged him again and he shook Hadley's hand. "As long as you don't hurt my brother again."

Fair enough, she thought, knowing it was the most she could expect from the most protective brother. The sad fact was, both she and Zach were destined to be hurt when her situation came to an end.

Once the conversation was over, Zach relaxed. The band began to play and the fireworks started soon after, alleviating the need for small talk. Hadley curled into Zach and enjoyed the spectacular explosions of color and sound, soaking it all in. And pushing Asher's too accurate comments away.

Afterwards, everyone said good night and left,

heading to their rooms at Serenity and Michael's or their respective houses. Hand in hand, she and Zach walked back to his house in comfortable silence. He locked up behind them and set the alarm.

She joined Zach, who was already in bed, after she finished washing up and brushing.

"I'm sorry Asher was such an ass," he said, patting the mattress for her to climb on.

She shrugged. "I don't blame him." Everything he'd said was true. She'd left and she would again. Obligations and her sister's life awaited her in Illinois. Suddenly chilled, she crossed her arms and rubbed her skin.

"Well, I do," Zach muttered. "My life is none of his business. Although…"

She narrowed her gaze. "What?"

He leaned against the pillows. "I get where he's coming from. Even though Dad was there for us after my biological mother left, as Asher got older, he assumed a parental role. That included creating Dirty Dare Vodka and ensuring we all invested and had money beyond what we earned in our jobs. Or trusts," he acknowledged, knowing the wealth made Hadley uncomfortable. "Falling in love with Nikki helped soften him but sometimes the asshole in him returns."

Hadley was unable to hold back her smile. "You are so lucky to have a family who will go to bat for you."

"The way you do for Dani."

She nodded.

"But who goes to bat for you?" Zach's serious gaze held hers. She was drawn into those gorgeous indigo eyes but she didn't want him feeling sorry for her.

"I can take care of myself." She always had.

"I'm serious. Who else looks out for you?" he asked.

"You do." She reached out a hand and cupped his cheek. "And I'm grateful." Her heart beat harder in her chest, her feelings for him almost too big to hold in.

"Not what I meant." He smiled but those eyes didn't sparkle back. "Hadley, who will take care of you when you go home?"

She swallowed hard. "We don't need to talk about this now."

His gaze narrowed, his mouth opened… and apparently he wasn't finished. "What's back in Illinois for you?"

Was he serious? "A career. Tenure at my school. Working off student loan forgiveness? Dani has her friends. Do you need more?" There was no Zach, none of his siblings, Sheila at the bar, Maddox, all people she was coming to know and like.

He clenched his jaw before answering. "I respect that. All of it. I'm just asking you to think about how you feel being here, where you have a more fulfilling life."

She shook her head. Her feelings didn't matter. Reality did. "Am I supposed to send Dani home to live with my father? Assuming he doesn't end up in prison? I'm not her legal guardian," she said, her voice rising.

"Okay." Zach held up both hands. "I understand. I'll back off," he said. "Please, just calm down. I didn't mean to upset you." He reached out and pulled her against him, holding her tight.

"I know you didn't." He just wanted something out of reach.

"And you're right. We don't need to get into this now. We have time," he said, sounding sad.

She nodded.

"Now you see why Asher is so protective. So don't be too hard on him. Your brother loves you."

And she did too.

The realization hit her hard and tears filled her eyes. She loved him and she couldn't keep him. All they had was now. She would never ask him to leave his family and businesses behind to move to Illinois. He was just as firmly entrenched in where he lived as she was.

"Hads? You okay?" he asked.

She covered her emotional reaction with a yawn. "Yes. Just tired."

His eyes crinkled as he studied her with concern. "It's been a long day. Let's get some sleep, okay?" He held out his arms and she slid into them.

Rolling over, she snuggled in, her back to his front so he could wrap himself around her from behind. And so she didn't have to face him and see all she had to lose.

Chapter Fifteen

A COUPLE OF days after the girls had scared Hadley to death, things had calmed down. Dani kept in touch more and was very contrite. It wasn't typical but she obviously realized how badly they had screwed up.

It was around eleven a.m. and Zach was about to head to work. Hadley was folding clothing she'd washed when she heard Zach's phone ring from the hall.

"Hello?" he said.

She finished with the last towel as he spoke.

"Yes. I'll be here. See you soon." He walked into the room and met her gaze. "Remy's stopping by with someone. They want to talk to you."

She stilled. "Why? What's going on?"

He drew a deep breath. "The man is a fed. They have information on your father." He picked up the empty laundry basket. "Come. We'll wait in the family room."

She walked to the oversize couch and sat down, waiting as Zach put the basket in the laundry room before joining her and taking a seat next to her.

She twisted her hands in her lap, her stomach churning, her nerves taking over. "You don't know what they want?" she asked.

He shook his head. "Remy asked me to be with you though," he said, grasping her hand. "Whatever the news, I'm with you, okay?"

She nodded. "Thank you." Her mind drifted to her father and the day she'd had to pack her things and run. She shook her head and sighed. "I don't know how my dad can put his kids through this much stress."

"Neither do I."

The doorbell rang, causing her stomach to give another nervous twist, as they both rose from their seats.

"I've got it," Zach said. "Stay here and relax."

She snorted. As if she could calm down.

Shaking his head, he strode out of the room and returned with Remy and a man in an ill-fitting tan suit. His hair was gray and receding, and he looked familiar.

Zach walked back to her, taking up a protective stance by her side. The tense look on Zach's face, the way his lips pulled into a tight line, scared her.

Remy walked up behind him and came to her side. "Hi, Hadley."

She treated him to a forced smile. "Remy."

"This is Sean Andrews. He works in the Violent

Crime and Racketeering section of the Justice Department," Remy said.

Andrews. Hadley narrowed her gaze. "I know you," she whispered.

He nodded. "Hello, Ms. Stevens. You've grown up."

Suddenly, she was thrust back to the night she'd been greeted by her father and two agents. One woman and... him. "You took us to Illinois."

He inclined his head. "Thank you for making the time to meet with me today," the federal agent said. "You did the right thing by taking your sister and leaving. Smart."

"Were you watching me?" she asked, horrified.

"No but we were keeping an eye on your father. We knew your action by extension of that." His cool demeanor was the same as when he'd blown up her world the first time.

She'd hated him then and she disliked him as much now. No compassion for the people whose lives he upended.

"How about we sit?" Zach asked, as if he knew she was about to lose it. He gestured around the room to the empty seats and the other men sat.

Zach placed a hand on her back, and she eased down onto the cushion with him by her side.

Agent Asshole leaned forward, facing her. "I'm

going to get right to it, Ms. Stevens. Your father has been arrested for fraud and money laundering conspiracy. A grand jury indicted him and his associates with one count of conspiracy to commit wire fraud, four counts of wire fraud and one count of conspiracy to commit money laundering."

She felt her eyes bulge and her lips part. Beside her, Zach moved closer and took her hand, but she'd gone numb.

The agent continued to talk. If he was aware of her emotional breakdown, he didn't care. "Without getting into details at the moment, you should know conspiracy to commit wire fraud has a possible penalty of five years in federal prison and convictions of wire fraud and conspiracy to commit money laundering have potential twenty-year prison sentences."

Nausea threatened and the important questions and words she knew she should say wouldn't come.

"We offered him a lesser charge if he turns on the masterminds who used the funds for their sex trafficking."

Sex trafficking. "Oh God. Those were the men who threatened to take me and Dani?" Her voice broke. As much as she'd known what her father was into, it hurt to hear it out loud.

The agent nodded. "It was a decent deal, but your father refused. It isn't a deal breaker for us convicting the other men, but it does make us have to work harder."

"I don't give a shit about your issues. Why the hell would my father turn down a deal for less time in prison?" she asked, her voice rising. "He has a daughter who needs a parent. He has to take the deal! I want to see him." She tried to push herself up from her seat, but Zach held on tight.

"Hads." He slipped an arm around her shoulders, holding her, his support unwavering. Zach's body felt warm against hers but inside she was ice cold.

"There's more. Let's get through it, okay?" Remy leaned forward, his expression full of regret.

She nodded, her throat full, tears dripping down her face. "Okay but first, can you arrange for me to see him?" She needed to convince him to turn so he might get out earlier. Anything to give her something to tell her sister that was positive. She'd given up on her dad when he'd risked his children a second time but she knew Dani still held out hope for him.

Agent Andrews shook his head. "I'm sorry but your father doesn't want to see you or your sister. He was insistent."

"Of course, he doesn't. He knows I'm going to try and convince him to do the right thing." As much as she hurt for herself, she was dying for Dani. How was she ever going to break this news to her sister?

She blinked and wiped her cheeks, trying to tell herself the tears were for Dani. But Hadley couldn't deny this whole situation had brought her back to the sixteen-year-old girl she'd been when her father had first upended her life.

"Can I at least send him a letter?" she asked.

Agent Andrews nodded. "I just can't promise he'll read it."

She drew a deep, steadying breath. "Does this mean it's over? We can go home?"

"I'm sorry, but you can't leave yet. We haven't picked up everyone involved, and your father owes them money, but we think we'll have them in custody soon. Once we round up the higher ups, we'll let you know. Then you can go back to your life."

Beside her, Zach had grown rigid. She understood. Pain sliced through her and nausea threatened at the thought of leaving him. But that had been the plan all along.

Reality dictated her choices and none of the reasons she needed to leave had changed. Except her father was in prison and her responsibilities when it came to Dani had increased tenfold. She was the sole adult in her sister's life. Dani's mother didn't count. And she had her own responsibilities.

She swallowed hard. "What about my sister? My father has sole custody. Dani's mother only has supervised visits."

The agent nodded. "Your father intends to sign over his full custodial rights to you."

Her chest hurt for her sister, but she nodded. She already took care of Dani but none of this would go down easy for a thirteen-year-old who loved her dad. Only Hadley was used to being let down by him.

"I realize this is a lot to take in. If Remy hadn't come to us, we'd be searching for you." He rose to his feet. "I'll be in touch when I have more information."

In a daze, she rose to her feet, barely aware of the goodbyes around her.

"DO YOU WANT to talk about it?" Zach and Hadley were now in the kitchen, their *guests* long gone.

Hadley hadn't said a word since the federal agent and Remy had left. Worried about Hadley, Zach had stayed home from work, afraid she might shatter at any moment.

"Hadley? I think you'd feel better if you let it out."

She turned to face him, her skin pale, her blue eyes glassy. "My father is going to prison. He can't afford a lawyer and if he won't turn on the people above him, he has *no* shot in hell of getting off."

Since everything she said was true, Zach remained

silent. Even though he could afford a lawyer who would try to keep the man out of prison, Zach wasn't convinced it was the best thing for Hadley and Dani. Keeping their old man locked up would mean his daughters were safe. At least, once the police arrested the guys they were looking for.

The fact was, even if the cops didn't find them, her father going to prison instead of turning meant they might leave his daughters alone, something Sean had mentioned when Zach walked him out. They just wanted more certainty before explaining things to Hadley.

"What am I going to tell Dani?" she asked, her voice still monotone.

"The truth? She's an older thirteen-year-old. She's seen and sensed the same things you have about your dad... scary men around the house, your father in a panic, forcing you to leave town. Dani is smart enough to know something big is going down."

Hadley nodded. "You're right. I just wish I could see my father and talk to him. But he won't see us."

He dipped his head before meeting her gaze. "I hate to say it, but maybe that's for the best. You can handle seeing him in prison. Dani probably can't, no matter how wise she is for her age."

She blew out a breath and nodded. "I know every-thing you're saying is true. And I can't put it off. Her mother is still out there, and I can't risk Dani hearing it from Patrice and not me."

He nodded "Why don't you give yourself a break and process everything. We can go tell Dani later."

Hadley let out a long breath and nodded. "I'm not looking forward to it."

He didn't blame her. "Do you want to go sit on the beach? At the pool? Relax inside and put on a movie?"

She shook her head, looking more vulnerable than he'd ever seen her. He slid closer, wanting to hold her, lend her his strength, and get her through this. "Then what *do* you want?" he asked.

"You."

She didn't have to ask twice.

He rose, bent, and scooped her into his arms. His girl needed to forget. And she *was* his. Whether she left or not, she'd always belong to him. Which meant he wasn't letting her go without a fight. He needed to convince her of how much he cared and now was the perfect time to start.

He strode through the house, into the bedroom, and laid her gently onto the bed. He stripped her of her leggings and T-shirt, what she called her hanging around the house clothes, leaving her naked on the bed.

As much as he wanted to take his time and lick his

way up her delectable body, he wanted to give her a connection to him more. He undressed just as quickly and lay down beside her, pressing his lips to hers and kissing her for a good long while.

Dipping his head, he licked around her nipple before pulling one into his mouth and sucking hard. She moaned and threaded her fingers through his hair, a move he loved even more when she scratched his scalp and tugged on his longish strands.

"I need you, Zach."

Her words and the emotion behind them were everything *he* needed.

He lifted his head and met her gaze. "And I want to give you what *you* need." He switched to her other breast, providing the same treatment. She tasted sweet, her moans even sweeter. He slid one finger through her slick wetness, making certain she was ready since her mind could be on all the different things causing her stress.

But he was happy to find her ready for him. He came over her and braced his arms on either side of her head. With his gaze on hers, he slid easily inside her warmth, neither breaking eye contact as he rocked into her. Instead of fast and furious, this was a slow coming together, more a reunion and a silent admission of unspoken feelings.

She raised her arms and he clasped her hands in

his, the slow pace as he dragged his cock out and eased back in had emotions he'd locked down years ago flooding back. He picked up speed with a steady thrusting until she rolled her hips and ground herself up and against him as she came.

Only then did he let himself go.

HADLEY STOOD BY Zach outside his parents' house as he rang their doorbell. She needed to focus on Dani and not the emotions making love with Zach had stirred.

Nothing mattered right now except telling her sister that her father was in prison, and would be staying there for the foreseeable future. Not even the fact that Hadley had just admitted to herself that she'd made love to Zach took precedence.

As they waited, he grabbed her hand and squeezed for reassurance. She glanced at him and smiled. He'd been her rock through all of this, and she was grateful.

The door opened and Serenity stood there, a surprised look on her face.

"Hi, Mom," Zach said.

"What are you two doing here? Not that I'm not happy to see you." She stepped aside and ushered them in with a sweep of her arm.

"I need to talk to Dani," Hadley said as they stepped into the foyer and Serenity shut the door behind them.

"Of course. I'll go get her. I think they're in Layla's room."

Serenity strode off and Zach turned Hadley towards him. "Are you okay?"

She shook her head. "I don't know what I am, but I do know you've been here for me through every step of this nightmare and… thank you."

He brushed a strand of hair off her cheek and tucked it behind her ear. She shivered as his hand caressed her skin. "You're going to get through this," he assured her. "I'll make sure of it."

"Layla Dare, come downstairs and tell your brother and Hadley what you just told me." Serenity sounded angrier than she'd been the night the girls had missed curfew, and she'd been furious then.

Hadley spun away from Zach. "What's wrong?" she asked as Serenity marched back into the room, a reluctant Layla trailing behind her.

Layla stepped forward. Her eyes were red and mascara ran down her face.

Something was very wrong. "Where's Dani?" Hadley asked, panic fueling the adrenaline in her veins.

Layla literally wrung her hands. "Umm… well…"

"Out with it," Serenity said in mom voice.

"Layla?" Zach's deep tone startled his sister.

"Dani has a secret phone and she's been talking to her mother," Layla said on a rush.

"What?" Hadley and Zach asked at the same time. He immediately put a calming hand on her shoulder, which she appreciated.

Layla shrugged. "She has a phone. She said her mom gave it to her the night before she came here but it's weird looking. Nothing like our iPhones."

Hadley blew out a deep breath, trying not to panic. "Where is Dani now?"

Biting down on her lower lip, Layla began to wring her hands again. "She went to meet her mom, but she was supposed to be back by now and she's not answering the number on her real phone."

Hadley spun to face Zach. "Oh my God. I never factored Patrice into the equation. That woman has always been trouble. Where could Dani be?"

Zach had already pulled out his cell. "I'm checking the tracker... Fuck. It's showing this address." He glanced at his sister, one eyebrow raised. "Tell me she didn't leave her phone here. That she was smart enough to bring it in case she needed us?"

"Zach." Hadley put her hand on his chest. "We already know the answer. The question is what are we going to do? How will we find her?" She held in her hysteria, knowing it would do no good. She needed to think clearly.

"Layla, do you know the phone number of the one she has on her?" Zach asked.

His sister glanced down, not lifting her head, obviously afraid to meet anyone's gaze.

"I'm sorry again," Serenity said. "I really thought the girls had learned their lesson. Layla was grounded and missed a big party." She put a hand on her daughter's shoulder. "What were you thinking?" she asked, more harshly.

"If I had to guess, Layla was returning the favor Dani did for her when they went to the bonfire without permission." As a teacher, Hadley knew teenagers.

Dani had been reckless, going off to see her mother, while Layla had been an adolescent who just didn't understand how serious things were. She was more sheltered and protected than Dani had ever been, which was why Hadley's anger was with her sister and not Layla. Friends protecting friends. She'd seen it over and over in her school.

"Is that the reason you didn't tell me?" Serenity asked.

Layla nodded. "She said she'd go see her mom and be home for dinner."

It was way past that time now and Hadley was having a more difficult time suppressing her worry.

Feeling dizzy, she needed a few minutes alone to think, so she could figure out why Patrice would have come to New York. Dani's mom had nothing to do with their father's dirty dealings. That Hadley knew of, anyway.

"I'll be right back," she murmured.

"Are you okay?" Zach asked, concern in his voice.

She nodded. "I just need a few minutes to think." She walked off towards the powder room and shut herself inside.

Turning on the faucet, she ran her wrists beneath the tap, letting the cold water shock her out of the fog of panic. She'd been through a lot in life but this worry for her sister had brought her to new heights of terror.

Her heart still thudded hard inside her chest but the black spots in front of her eyes receded, the dizziness passing. At least she could concentrate again.

From inside her bag, her cell rang, and she dug through it quickly, retrieving the phone.

Unknown Number showed on the screen.

Her hand shook as she swiped to answer and put the cell up to her ear. "Hello?"

"Hadley?"

"Who is this?" she asked, the dizziness returning.

"Someone you want to listen to. You've caused me a lot of trouble by leaving town and disappearing."

She swallowed hard. "Why? I don't even know

who you are."

"Let's just say you have something that I want and now, I have something that *you* want."

"Hads, this guy's my mom's boyfriend though from what I've heard I think he's her dealer." Dani's voice sounded in the background.

"Put a muzzle on your kid," he barked in a tone that turned Hadley's blood cold.

She gasped. "Put my sister on the phone!"

"You're not calling the shots. I am. Meet me at the impound lot where your car is located. Once I check and make sure my packages are still there, we'll swap valuables. *Then* you can talk to your sister. And come alone."

"Impound lot?" He disconnected the call before she could say more.

Oh my God. He had Dani. Her own mother had something to do with her kidnapping. Hadley broke into a sweat as questions rose in her brain.

Why would Patrice use her daughter?

What did they want from Hadley's car?

She braced her hands on the counter by the sink and stared into the mirror, as if looking at her reflection would provide answers. The one thing she knew was that he'd said to come alone and she needed to go. Now. But how was she was going to ditch Zach and get to New York City, to an impound lot whose location she didn't know? But Zach did.

Though she trusted him, she needed to do what Patrice's boyfriend wanted, or risk Dani's life.

A knock sounded on the door, and she immediately opened it to find Zach standing there, his forehead wrinkled, worry in his expression. "I'm just checking on you. You were gone awhile. Mom and Layla went upstairs so my sister could get lectured. And we need to talk about the next steps to find Dani."

Hadley nodded. "I'm okay." She looked into his indigo eyes and quickly glanced away. She couldn't look at him and lie. "I thought..." she trailed off.

What?

She thought she'd what? Find her sister on her own? But she had to. She'd been ordered to come alone. The words came back to her along with the implied threat behind them.

"I don't know. I'm shaken up but I'm fine," she said.

He lifted her hands. "You're not. You're trembling and I don't blame you. But we *will* figure out where your sister is."

She swallowed hard. She ought to tell him everything. After all, she'd come to Zach for help, and she knew him better than to think he'd let anything happen to Dani. Still, she hesitated, her thoughts all over the place but when it came down it, there was no way she could handle this alone.

She looked back into his eyes and her composure broke. "I'm not okay. Not only is Dani missing but I just got a call from someone who has her. He said to meet him by the impound lot where my car is." She let the words out in a rush before she could change her mind.

"Fuck." He ran a hand through his hair.

"There's more. He said to come alone but I don't know where the lot is. Or what they want. Or who they are. I've been trying to figure out what to do."

His eyes narrowed. "Hadley, you aren't alone anymore. *We* are going to figure out what to do."

She blew out a relieved breath and nodded. "Right. Thank you. I guess between being ordered to come alone and me being used to handling things alone, I panicked."

He nodded but she caught the hurt in his eyes. She should have rushed out to him right after getting the call. "Zach, I'm sorry."

He gave her a curt nod. "Let's go." He turned and strode out of the bathroom, and she followed.

"Where are we going?" she asked.

"To the impound lot." He had his phone in his hand and was tapping away.

"What are you doing?" she asked, rushing alongside him to the car in his parents' driveway.

He was still focused on the screen. "Getting Remy working on who called you but I'm assuming it's a burner and we'll get nothing."

Next thing she knew, they were back in the car and headed to Manhattan.

Chapter Sixteen

Z ACH EXCEEDED THE speed limit the entire trip to the city. He pulled into the impound lot, his fingers tight around the steering wheel, his knuckles white. With more questioning on the ride, Hadley told him she'd heard Dani's voice and her sister had yelled out that the guy was her mother's sleazy boyfriend.

He wasn't sure if Patrice being involved was better for Dani, that her mother would protect her, or worse because it showed she didn't care about her daughter, only herself. He assumed the latter. And that was why he wanted the kid back ASAP, he thought, as he put the car in park.

No sooner had he shut off the engine than Hadley reached for the handle, but he made sure the door lock button was engaged.

"Wait."

She turned to him. "Are you kidding? The longer I do, the longer Dani's in that crazy person's hands."

He slid a hand behind the back of her headrest. "That crazy person says you have something he wants in your car. That means you have the upper hand. Now take a deep breath and stay calm. We'll get out of the car and if no one approaches you, we'll go search your vehicle."

"We?" her voice echoed throughout the car. "He said to come alone. Do you want to get Dani hurt? It's bad enough you're here with me."

He stiffened at what felt like a rejection. Rationally, he understood. Emotionally, he felt turned upside down. He couldn't deny her questioning whether or not to tell him about the phone call stung. He thought they were at the point where she automatically trusted him. He'd been wrong. With no choice, he put his issues with Hadley on the back burner until they got Dani home.

Focusing on the main issue, he cleared his throat. "Upper hand, remember? Let's go find out what's in the car," he said and unlocked the doors. After climbing out, he strode around to her side of the car, not wanting Hadley unprotected for a second.

Before leaving for the city, he'd stopped home. He'd been wearing shorts and told Hadley he needed to run inside to change into jeans. He also wanted his gun, which he tucked into his waistband holster with a T-shirt and a long sleeve button-down over it.

No way was he going into a situation with two drug addicts unarmed. He'd also called Remy, who still had friends on the force, to arrange for back up if things went down on the street outside the lot. Remy's family name and former status in the department held a lot of weight and he let Zach know via text he'd handled everything on his end.

In addition, Remy had information for Hadley. The feds had arrested the higher ups in her father's case in a sting that had been going on at the same time Hadley was being informed about her father's arrest. Something Zach told her on the trip into Manhattan. She deserved to have one less thing on her mind as they went to retrieve her sister. Neither Zach nor Hadley discussed the implications. She was free to return home. They were too focused on Dani.

The street the lot was located on was empty and quiet. Zach hooked one arm around Hadley's waist as they walked up to the door. He buzzed and they were let in. He approached the window where a young man sat leaning back in his seat, his legs propped on the counter.

Zach cleared his throat.

The guy swung his feet down to the floor and swept his too-long hair off his forehead. "What do ya need?" he asked.

"Dario around?" Zach looked beyond him but the door behind the guy was shut. Dario was expecting him. He, too, had been alerted since having drugs in his garage would, in other circumstances, land him in jail. He also needed to know that if things went right, the cops would be swarming the place.

He was relieved nobody had approached them before they got to the car. It made it easier for them to search the car without the dirtbag breathing down their necks.

"Yo, D! Got someone asking for you," the guy yelled.

A few minutes later, Dario, the manager of the lot walked out from the rear. About Zach's age, he and Dario had gotten to know each other thanks to the amount of cars towed from The Back Door's lot after being left for a stretch.

"Zach! It's been too long." Dario strode over and slapped him on the back, pulling him in for a hug and tucking something inside his jacket pocket. As planned.

His blond hair had been shaved last time Zach had seen him and now he had begun growing it back. "Who's this pretty lady?" Dario asked.

Zach eased Hadley closer. "This is Hadley. Hadley, meet Dario."

"Hi." She treated him to a stiff greeting. He knew she was worried about Dani, but he couldn't let on to Hadley that he had a plan.

Talking to the lot owner was part of his usual routine. "I heard you have my girl's car?"

Dario inclined his head. He flipped Zach the keys.

"Come with me." He led them through the door he'd come through and into the back, bypassing going outside. He opened the metal, over-sized garage door. Zach didn't mind not hearing the loud, grinding gears.

"First floor in the back. No charge. Just keep my drinks free."

Zach chuckled. "Will do."

Dario grinned. "I'll go open the electric door so you can pull out."

"Thanks, man. But we're not going to take it just yet. I want to grab something Hadley left inside and once she makes her plans, we'll be back for the car. That work for you?"

Dario nodded. "Head on inside and let me know when you're finished."

Zach waited until Dario stepped back through the door to the offices and closed it behind him before turning to Hadley.

Bracing his hands on her shoulders, he let her know the next steps. "Okay, if Patrice's boyfriend was watching, he hasn't shown his face. Right now, let's dig through the vehicle. Once we find what he's after, we walk outside where I assume he'll be waiting."

As would the cops Remy had called. Not wanting to give Hadley more to worry about, he hadn't told her what his plan was. He didn't want her any jumpier than she was or for her to accidentally give something away.

She drew a shaky breath and met his gaze, fear obvious in her wide eyes. "Promise me you have a plan?"

He nodded. "I promise. And I will do the best I can to get your sister home and safe with you again."

"That's good enough for me," she said in a shaky voice. "I trust you and I'm sorry if I made you feel like I didn't."

The fist around his heart that had been squeezing him tight loosened. "And that's good enough for me. Come on." He grasped her hand and together they walked to her car.

Ignoring the muggy heat and humidity in the garage, they found her old vehicle. He opened the locks. She crawled into the back, and he took the front. He turned over floor mats, dug his hand between and beneath the seats, opened the glove compartment and sorted through every paper inside. He delved into the center panel, the door wells and in the back, Hadley did the same.

"Nothing." She smacked the seats in frustration.

"Come out." He pushed himself backwards out of the car and met her around the back. "I'll pop the trunk."

Once it opened, they both began to search. "This is quite the mess," he said, tossing through sweatshirts and bags filled with who knew what.

She let out a laugh. "All the stuff from my classroom that I never got a chance to empty out when I got home. Posters from the walls, markers, dry erase markers..." She shrugged. "Normally I'd already be buying more for next year."

He heard the warmth in her voice and turned his head. "You love to teach, don't you?"

She nodded. "I do."

Was he delusional in thinking he could convince her to do the work she loved here? He couldn't begin to consider the future until he fixed the present.

Digging his fingers beneath the cargo mat, he lifted it up and... "Damn." He pulled out a heavy bag of what looked like crystal meth. Grabbing the carpet again, he ripped it off and revealed three more weighty bags of drugs.

She sucked in a loud breath. "Is that..."

"Meth," he said, placing the bag back down.

Hadley leaned heavily against the car. "Oh my God. I've been thinking ever since that call, and now I can put the pieces together." She swiped her arm over her glistening forehead. "The day we left home, Dani didn't want to go. She said her mother was coming to visit and I reminded her she'd just seen her mother the night before. I didn't add that Patrice rarely kept her word. But it was weird, her telling Dani she'd come back the next night."

"And now we know that she needed to return because she'd stashed these in your car. Probably for her drug-dealing boyfriend."

"Holy shit. I drove here with bundles of meth in my car!" she said, her voice rising. "What if I'd been pulled over?"

Zach reached for her and yanked her against him, wrapping his arms around her waist. "Breathe. It's almost over."

"I'm going to kill Patrice," Hadley said through gritted teeth.

Get in line, Zach thought. But neither would have that chance if things went as planned.

Before heading out, Zach checked his phone and read a quick rundown of the plan from Remy. His partner had pulled off miracles, utilizing his cop contacts and the feds, who'd met with Dario before Zach got to the city.

Dario had already planted a listening device on Zach when he'd hugged him earlier, having been given one by the cops before Zach got to the city. They'd be listening to everything that went down.

Zach was ready.

Now they just needed luck on their side.

ZACH HELD ONE of Hadley's reusable grocery bags with a package of drugs inside. The rest he left in the locked car, assuring her not to worry. He'd tried his damndest to get her to stay in Dario's office, but she was going to be there for her sister. Besides, the dirtbag had called *her*. So, she was all in. If Zach hadn't given in to her pleas, they'd still be arguing.

He held Hadley close with his free arm and they headed out, pausing by the office to let Dario know they were leaving. Once outside, her heart was pounding so hard she swore she heard the sound. Across the street was a heavily treed, abandoned-looking park with a chain link fence and signs dangling off it.

No sooner had they walked out to the sidewalk and turned than a man appeared around the nearest street corner. Wearing a baseball cap and a zippered hoodie, despite the heat, he approached them, and Zach stopped, keeping her close.

"What part of come alone did you not understand?" he asked, hands in his front pockets, his body jerking while he kept his distance.

"Where's Dani?" Zach asked. He deliberately ignored the question.

He shrugged, taking a step back. Zach followed with Hadley, one step closer.

"You obviously already retrieved the merchandise, also not part of the plan. I said to meet me outside so I could go in and check the car. Where's the rest of my shit?"

"You don't expect me to carry it all out, do you? Now let me see Dani. Then I'll give you the bag and the keys to get the rest," Zach said.

The guy moved from foot to foot, antsy and jittery, his hands shaking. He was obviously hopped up on drugs.

"Lady, you are a pain in the ass," he said, speaking to her and not Zach. "First, I couldn't get the damn drugs because the Mob was coming and going from your house, then the cops were all over fucking place. *Then* I find out you left the damn state... with my product," he said, voice rising.

Zach tried to push Hadley behind him, but she refused to move. She wanted her sister.

"Bitch! I was beaten because of you. The guy I owed wasn't happy to find out I didn't have hundreds of thousands of dollars worth of shit, as promised." He pulled off his hood to reveal fading bruises on his sallow skin. "You ever try driving to the city with a broken rib?"

Obviously he liked to talk, a byproduct of being hyped up. She swallowed hard, sensing Zach was letting him babble until he'd calmed down enough to focus.

"Come on. Make the trade like you promised,"

Zach urged him.

"Hey, Patty! This asshole thinks he's calling the shots," the guy yelled out, laughing with a high pitched voice, tilting his head back toward the direction from which he'd came.

"That's because I am. You need what we have." Zach stood still as he spoke, his coolness under pressure impressive since she was as jumpy as the dealer.

But Hadley also had enough. If Patrice was here, then so was her sister. She hoped. "I want my sister now." Her steady voice surprised her.

Zach stiffened at her intervening.

"Hads?" Dani screamed.

"I'm here!" she yelled back.

Zach held her tighter. "Do not move," he warned under his breath. "I don't need him attacking you."

"Mom, let me go!" Dani shrieked.

"Can't you keep the bitch quiet?" The boyfriend yelled. "She hasn't shut her fucking mouth since she showed up."

God, her sister was going to give Hadley a heart attack. Of course, she couldn't be a quiet hostage.

"Dani, stay calm," Zach called out.

"I told you to gag her again." The man who stood between Hadley and her sister was twitching as he spoke, body parts unable to remain still.

"I'm hungry! You said you'd feed me if I was quiet, and you haven't. Hadley?" Despite the bravado, Dani's voice shook.

But she was brave, obviously wanting to let Hadley know she was here and okay, but who knew if Patrice had a weapon or how desperate she was.

Hadley wanted to believe she'd never hurt her child but by using her as bait and leverage, she'd already done just that. Hadley was sweating, her neck damp, her hands wet, her entire body rigid with fear for her sister.

"Patrice, do the right thing and send Dani out to me. Please." She wasn't above begging.

"Don't you dare let her go!" The dealer pulled a gun from his pocket and Hadley took a shocked step back. He couldn't keep his body from shaking. The gun could go off any minute.

"Whoa. No reason for that," Zach said in a calm tone. "Here. Take the drugs." Zach tossed them so they fell in front of the guy's feet.

He bent forward, grabbing the bag. "Now give me keys so I can get the rest, deliver them and get my cut before I end up dead in the East River." He continued to twitch and jerk as he spoke, the gun waving wildly.

The moment Zach pulled out his keys, all hell broke loose. Police officers came from seemingly out of nowhere, jumping the fence across the street, a sea of blue shocking Hadley.

Zach shoved her against the wall, blocking her with his body. The brick scraped her hands and her shoulder hurt but she remained still, not fighting him and praying the crazy tweaked up dealer didn't shoot and hit him.

"Clear!" Hadley heard the cops yell.

"It's okay," Zach said, his voice warm in her ear. He stepped back and helped her balance herself.

"Oh my God." She glanced around. Tweaker guy was on his knees, hands cuffed behind his back. "Where's Dani?"

"There." Zach put his hands on her shoulders and turned her towards the corner. An officer guided Patrice toward them on the sidewalk, her hands also behind her back.

Dani turned the corner next with another officer by her side. "Hadley!" she screamed and came running, slamming into Hadley full force.

Hadley wrapped her arms around her sister and let the tears flow. Burying her face in Dani's hair, she inhaled the teen's fading perfumed scent and squeezed tight. "Oh my God. Tell me you're okay!"

She pulled her sister away and looked her over from head to toe. Other than wrinkled shorts and T-shirt and puffy eyes, she seemed unharmed.

"I'm okay. I wasn't kidding that I'm starving. And

is it true that Dad's in prison? Mom said he's never getting out."

Hadley closed her eyes and groaned. "I—"

Before she could answer, Zach cleared his throat. "Hey, Dani."

She looked up at him with wide eyes. "I'm sorry, Zach."

He shook his head. "Nobody blames you for going when your mom called though I'm sure your sister will have a set of new rules for you to follow."

Hadley managed a grin.

"I'm not sorry for that, okay well I am, but I meant, I'm sorry for saying you were a jerk who couldn't help us that day I met you in the city." She brushed the pink stripe of hair out of her face.

He coughed, then narrowed his gaze. "I don't remember you saying that."

"Me neither." Hadley shot her sister a warning glare despite the trauma she'd just been through.

Dani shrugged. "Oh. Well, then I thought it and I'm sorry. You were awesome today. You too, Hads."

She hugged her sister again. "I have to admit I was scared to death. And Zach's right. We have a lot to talk about when we get home."

A man in a jacket strode over to them. "Excuse me. I'm Detective Benjamin Rodell and I need to question everyone. Including the young lady."

Hadley straightened her shoulders. "The *young lady* was the victim of a crime, and she's a minor and I'm not leaving her alone."

Zach put a hand on Hadley's shoulder, and she appreciated his support. "Come on, Rodell," he said. "She's a kid and she's been traumatized. We'll make her available but not now."

The man who Zach obviously knew frowned. "You and Remy might have been running your own op again, but you're no longer in charge."

"Remy called his precinct and the NYPD understood the emergency. If he'd trusted you, he'd have pulled you in."

Hadley listened to the two men, confused. "What's going on?"

"I'll explain later," Zach promised.

"I want to talk to my daughter." Patrice yelled loudly from where she stood cuffed outside a patrol car.

Hadley stiffened.

"No!" Dani threw herself at Hadley, wrapping her arms around her waist. "I don't want to be with her. Don't make me. She was mean. She yelled at me. She slapped me when I argued because I didn't want them to hurt you."

Hadley met Zach's gaze over her sister's head, narrowing her gaze to let him know what she thought of

Dani's words. "I want Dani out of here."

"Not yet—"

"Shut up, Rodell or I'm going to your chief as a concerned citizen. You know how he feels about his detectives not taking the victim into account. Especially underaged ones who need to be seen by a doctor."

Zach turned a warmer gaze to Hadley. "I've got this. Patrice won't bother her." He turned and strode to where the police held both Patrice and her dirtbag boyfriend, the detective following him.

A few seconds later, both were being pushed into the back of separate patrol cars with officers' hands on their heads as they climbed in.

Hadley let out a relieved breath. When she'd come to Zach, it had been on a whim, a desperate move she'd hoped was the right one. She hadn't known how skilled he was or how far his influence reached.

"Dani?"

Her sister released her and stepped back. Her eyes were red and her hair fell into her face. Hadley handed her a hair tie she kept around her wrist.

"Thanks," Dani said, as she pulled the long strands into a bun on top of her head.

"Honey, were you hurt? I mean seriously, not being hungry, not putting on that bravado you like so much. Did Patrice do more than slap you?"

"She gagged me with a disgusting bandana thing,"

she said in a shaky voice. "No one's ever hit me before. And she's my mom." The tears welled in her eyes and Hadley wanted to march over to Patrice and wrap her hands around the woman's neck.

"Nobody will ever hurt you again." Speaking of being hurt… Hadley put an arm around Dani's shoulder. "Did your mom's boyfriend touch you at all?" she asked gently. "You can tell me anything." She held her breath, waiting for an answer.

Looking down, Dani shook her head. "I know what you're asking and no." She wrapped her arms around herself tight.

"Anything else?"

Another head shake.

Okay, so maybe some trauma therapy would be necessary but thank God there was nothing more.

Zach cleared his throat.

Hadley hadn't heard him approach.

"I let my parents and Layla know Dani is okay," he said.

To Hadley's surprise, Dani looked up and met his gaze. "I'm sorry I made Layla lie for me."

"When did your mom give you the phone?" Hadley asked, curious.

Dani shrugged. "A while ago. In case I ever wanted to talk to her… or get away from you, she said. But I didn't see any harm in it. It's not like I would ever run away from you... except today I hadn't seen Mom in so long and she said she missed me. That she'd come to the city just to see me and take me for lunch, and we never did that together." She sniffed and wiped her eyes with her arm. "She said not to tell you. That it was our special secret."

Understanding the pull of needing to be wanted by her mom, Hadley nodded. Patrice had played Hadley and Dani, but she'd used her teenage daughter in ways that were unforgiveable.

"Out of curiosity, how did you get here?" Zach asked.

Dani let out a sigh. "Layla lent me money. She called for the Uber and once I was in the city, I took a taxi to the address Mom gave me."

Hadley closed her eyes and shook her head. So much could have gone wrong. Worse than what had actually happened, which was pretty scary to begin with.

"Okay, ladies. I said we'd stay in the city and come by the station so we could all give statements. Dani, we should get you checked out by a doctor when we get home."

She shook her head. "I'm fine. I don't need a doctor."

Zach glanced at Hadley.

She bit the inside of her cheek and shook her head,

meaning they'd talk about it later. Zach was right. When they got back to the Hamptons, her sister was getting seen and checked over.

"Okay since we have to stick around for a bit, how about we go get Dani something to eat before we go do our thing at the police station?"

Dani's head perked up at the mention of food. "Yes! I'm starving! Mom said lunch so I didn't eat anything before I left, and nobody gave me food or water."

Zach shook his head, his grin wide, now that Dani was back to her old self, at least on the surface. "Sounds like they kept you in prison."

"Might as well have been," Dani muttered. "Speaking of prison, if Dad's locked up like Mom said, and she's probably going to jail too, what's going to happen to me?" she asked in a small voice Hadley never wanted to hear again.

She grabbed her sister's hand. "You're with me, just like always."

She didn't bother explaining their father would have to sign over custody. That would hurt. Hell, it hurt Hadley just to hear it, too. But she didn't want Dani worrying at all.

Dani remained quiet.

"You want to be with me, right?"

With a nod, she gave Hadley a tight squeeze again,

holding on as if she'd never let go. Hadley rubbed her hand over her messy bun. "Everything's going to be okay, sis. We're a team. You and me."

After a few seconds, Zach cleared his throat. "It's hot as hell out here and *someone* said they were hungry."

Dani perked up and they walked back to Zach's car, leaving Hadley alone with her thoughts.

The danger was over. She and Dani were safe. Hadley knew what that meant. Her time with Zach had come to an end.

Chapter Seventeen

ONCE ZACH DROVE them home, late thanks to the length of time it took for them all to make their official statements, Dani asked to stay with Hadley. Zach's heart broke for the teen who, in one day, had lost both her father and her mother. The only silver lining for Dani was Hadley. She'd always been her rock and that wouldn't ever change.

He turned down the covers and slid into bed alone. Hadley was in the guestroom with her sister. They had a lot to talk about and for all her bravado, Dani was still just a scared kid. He expected Hadley to sleep in her sister's room and was shocked when the bedroom door opened, and she walked inside.

Wearing a long, pale pink, V-neck sleepshirt, he couldn't help but be drawn to the outline of her breasts and nipples beneath. His cock reacted but now wasn't the time. Though he and Hadley hadn't been alone since rescuing Dani, he knew what came next and his gut churned at the thought of her telling him they were leaving.

"Hey," she said, walking over to the bed and collapsing on *her* side.

"How's Dani?" he asked, worried about the teen.

Hadley lowered the covers and sat down, pushing herself up against the pillows before turning to face him. "Asleep, thank goodness. We talked and I believe her when she says Tony didn't touch her *that way*." She shuddered at the thought.

"Thank fuck."

They'd learned the dirtbag boyfriend's name from Dani and Zach hoped he got the ass-kicking he deserved once he was permanently locked up. Unless he wanted to fight the charges, but Zach assumed he'd turn on the bigger guys for a lesser sentence. He didn't want Dani near a courtroom. She'd had enough trauma.

"I thought you were going to stay with her tonight?"

Hadley sighed. "I was going to. I figured she'd be wired but she fell asleep so fast and is out cold. She'll come find me if she needs me."

Leaning against the pillow, she faced him, exhaustion evident in the dark circles beneath her eyes. "You should get some sleep, too."

She nodded, her eyelids half-mast already.

"Come here." He held out an arm and she slipped into his arms. Pulling her close, he wrapped her tight and they lay in comfortable silence.

His heart beat hard in his chest but apparently, tonight wasn't going to include the conversation he dreaded.

He breathed into her hair and suppressed a groan.

He loved her. He loved her irrepressible sister. And he wanted them both here in his house and in his life. In the morning, he intended to out his feelings and ask her to stay.

He didn't want to let her go but he respected her enough to accept her final decision. He just hoped she didn't gut him in the process.

HADLEY WOKE UP early. Zach slept beside her. He'd rolled onto his stomach but had one arm over her waist. She couldn't help the smile that tugged at her lips at how he always touched her in his sleep. Tears followed because they needed to talk and she didn't know how to say the words she needed to say.

Slipping out of bed, she went to the bathroom, did her thing, brushed her teeth, and headed back to bed, finding Zach awake and waiting for her. The covers fell to his waist, revealing his delicious abs, tanned skin, and muscular arms, folded across his chest.

Her mouth watered at the sight. God, she was going to miss him.

He patted the space beside him, and she walked

over and climbed in. Meeting her gaze, he spoke first. "Let's do this. It won't get easier if we avoid the conversation."

She nodded and swallowed hard. "Me first, okay?" She'd been going over it in her head as best she could.

He gestured for her to speak.

She took his hand and squeezed tight, holding on as she spoke. It was ironic that she counted on him to give her the courage to leave him.

"I never thought we'd have a second chance. Even when I saw your picture in the magazine, coming here was an act of desperation." She swiped her tongue over her dry lips. "But you agreed to help. You took us into your home, your life. And I fell in love with you all over again."

His eyes opened wide, flaring with hope she hadn't meant to give.

She shook her head. "But love isn't enough. As a teenager, I thought it was. Our love got me through a shitty life. Holding onto my feelings for you helped get me through the early years in Illinois. But I'm an adult now and I know better." She blinked and the tears she'd been holding back flowed.

"Baby—"

"I need to get this out, okay? I'm Dani's guardian now. Legally, officially, I'm all she has, and her home, her life is somewhere else." She sniffed and wiped her cheeks with her free hand. "And so is mine."

At least she thought it was. Her job, commitments, the ways she agreed to pay off her education loans. She didn't have a lot of close friends, just teacher acquaintances because she always needed to be around for her sister. Like a parent would have been. She didn't meet them for drinks or go out on the weekends. But she had a life she'd created, and she needed to go back.

"My turn?" he asked.

No sooner did she nod than his hand whipped out, grabbed behind her neck, and he pulled her in for a kiss. A long, delectable, wet kiss. One full of need.

By the time he released her, her belly was heavy, her sex throbbed, and desire pulsed through her body. "Zach—"

"Nope. My turn." He sat up straighter, his gaze never leaving hers. "You can have a life here. You and Dani. She has a room here she can decorate however she wants. I know that's important to teenage girls." His lips lifted in a grin. "You two are a package deal and I love that. You're independent and I respect that, too. We can work out the logistics of how you can teach here in New York. We can make anything work. If you want it to. Baby, I *want* you to stay."

Her throat was so full she couldn't speak. The tears just continued to fall. "I always told you I had to go back when the danger passed."

He braced his hands on her shoulders. "And now I'm telling you, stay here with me."

"Don't you get it?" she asked, forcing the words past the huge lump in her throat. "From the day I was pulled into WITSEC, I've been told where to go, what to say, who to be. Now I need to go home and find out where I belong. Where Dani and I belong. And I won't know for sure unless I go back." She couldn't say go home because she feared her home was right here.

But she needed to find out.

Pain etched his expression, his cheekbones seeming sharper as he pulled in a breath. "Then you need to leave, but know that back then? I would have gone anywhere with you, if I only knew where to find you."

She sniffed, her nose threatening to run along with her weepy eyes. "We were kids. And now we're adults with responsibilities."

"I want you and Dani to be *my* responsibility, but you're right. I'm stuck here with two businesses, and I have no right to ask *you* to make the sacrifice to stay. But I'm asking anyway. Even though I know you're going to say no."

She brought her hands up to cup his face, memorizing each feature. "I do have to go, and figure out the right thing to do for Dani, and for me."

He nodded. "Then know you're taking my heart with you." Before she could reply, he rolled her onto her back, coming down on top of her and in minutes, he was inside her, probably for the last time.

Chapter Eighteen

S INCE THE POLICE had taken Hadley's car as evidence, the next morning, Zach drove her to a car rental place where she picked up a vehicle to take her and Dani to Illinois.

After saying a difficult goodbye to Zach, Hadley and Dani stopped by Serenity and Michael Dare's house to do the same, and to thank them for all their help. Dani and Layla cried as only teenagers could, loudly, as they promised to keep in touch and stay friends forever.

Hadley and Dani arrived back at their house late in the day, almost forty-eight hours after leaving the Hamptons. They'd stopped at a hotel for a night, this time at a nice place Hadley was able to put on her credit card. They deserved a comfortable night together and she let Dani order room service and watch a movie on the TV. Her sister got lost in the story, but Hadley's mind was on Zach.

The entire trip, she had a gnawing pain in her stomach, one that told her she was making a mistake. Even so, she needed to go home and make permanent decisions from there. Zach had called his attorney, who promised to work on finalizing custody papers for Hadley and Dani, to make sure they were permanent. Even if their father walked out of prison one day before Dani turned eighteen, Hadley wasn't giving him control of her sister's well-being.

As Hadley turned into the driveway, Dani craned her neck to look at the house she'd always called home. "This place is a dump!"

Shocked by the comment, Hadley slammed on the breaks and thank goodness the seatbelts held them in place. "Jesus." She put the car park in stared at her sister. "Are you kidding? Just because you spent a month in the Hamptons doesn't mean you should judge what we can afford."

Dani glanced down. "You're right and I'm sorry. It's just a shock compared to the Dares' homes."

No kidding, Hadley thought. The house *was* a dump. If they stayed, maybe she could afford a nicer condo. "Let's go inside and we can come back for our bags. I want to make sure the AC is working and see how Dad left everything." She prayed he hadn't lived like a complete messy hoarder while they had been gone, and Hadley wasn't around to clean.

Together they climbed out of the car, walked up the overgrown path, the weeds coming through between each bluestone step. Hadley had her keys in her hand and let them in... to find the entire place trashed.

"Holy shit!" Dani said from behind her.

Hadley sighed, suddenly not having the strength to correct her sister's language.

"Who did this?" she asked, following Hadley inside.

"My best guess? Someone looking for your mother's drugs, our father's... whatever, or the FBI or police. I don't know." But it was on her to clean it up.

After a quick view of every room, Hadley knew they couldn't stay there until she could get the place in some sort of order. The couches had been shredded, the mattresses too. The kitchen items were all over the floor and even the bathrooms were unusable, toiletries tossed everywhere. "Looks like we're going to a hotel again tonight."

"More room service?" Dani asked.

Hadley shrugged. "Why not?" Her phone buzzed inside her handbag, and she pulled it out to take a look.

Zach: Did you get home safely?

She smiled at his thoughtful question and the fact that he hadn't just written her off because she'd decided to leave.

Though, more and more, she wondered why the hell she believed she could have any kind of life here. Dani either.

She replied, omitting the details about the house. He'd worry and insist on coming to help her. This was her problem, not his. He'd done enough for her already.

"What's with the smile? Is that Zach?" Dani asked.

"Yeah." Perceptive kid. Then again, who else could it be? She hadn't heard from any of her local friends since she'd disappeared.

"Tell him I said hi," she said.

Hadley nodded. "I will. Now, come on. Let's go find a decent place to stay." They walked out and she locked up the house.

Hours later, they were ensconced in a hotel room with double beds. They'd eaten in the room, both indulging in hamburgers and French fries. Dani had added a chocolate shake.

Hadley finished up in the bathroom and walked out, wearing a nightshirt, and she settled into bed. Since Dani was still watching a show on TV, Hadley lay back and closed her eyes. As she'd expected, her time in New York came back to her like a movie reel. From walking into the bar and seeing Zach for the first time to the first family meal with his parents and siblings, tutoring Maddox's brother, working at the restaurant, and, of course, making love with Zach.

Her body tingled at the memory. But other memories surfaced too. Dani knowing about Zach being her high school boyfriend and that mortifying vibrator comment at the Dare family dinner.

Hadley sat up in bed. "Dani!"

"What?" Her sister turned toward her.

"Just how did you know about me leaving Zach before prom?" Hadley knew she'd never told her that story.

Dani's face flushed red. "I… umm… might have gone looking in your closet and found your old diaries."

Hadley had been an avid diary keeper after she'd been uprooted. She blinked, staring at her sister. "And you *read* them?"

She wrinkled her nose. "Maybe? I knew I shouldn't have but I was just so curious. You mentioned having an old boyfriend once, but you were so vague, and I was curious. I'm sorry!" she said, covering her eyes with her hands.

Good God, the kid was a drama queen. "And how did you know I had vibrators in my drawer?"

"Would you believe I was putting away your laundry? Okay! I wanted to try on one of your pretty bras and I found it."

Instead of being angry, Hadley burst out laughing, grateful for the light moment after the trying last week they'd had.

She shook her head and when Dani removed her

hands from her face, she grinned. "So, you're not mad?"

"Just ask next time, okay?"

Dani nodded. "Hads?"

"What?"

She looked around the hotel room. "What are we going to do?"

"Clean up the house? Maybe put it up for sale?"

Dani flopped back against the pillows. "And then what?"

"Maybe move into a condo?"

"Or go back to the Hamptons?" Dani asked at the same time.

Shock rippled through her. "You'd want to leave here? What about your friends?"

Biting down on her nail, Dani lifted one shoulder "I kind of stopped texting with them. Or they stopped texting me. I think they forgot about me while I was gone."

Hadley sighed. This kid had been through so much. "I'm sure you'll pick right up where you left off. Like when some of your friends went away to sleep away camp. Same thing."

"What about Zach?" Dani asked.

Hadley's heart squeezed at the question and the mention of his name. "What about him?"

"Did you really want to leave?"

It was Hadley's turn to shrug. "I thought it was the right thing to do. I have responsibilities here. My job. The house. And you had school and your friends." She paused to think. "I just wanted to do right by you. Your mom and dad aren't going to be in your life anymore and I didn't want more upheaval for you."

"What about *your* life, Hads? Don't you love him?"

Her heart began to beat harder in her chest. "Yeah. I do."

"Then why are we here?" Dani asked.

Tears filled Hadley's eyes as she replied. "I really don't know."

★   ★   ★

"TO THE DARE brothers." Nick raised his glass.

Asher, Harrison, and Zach followed, clinking their glasses together. "Why don't we do this more often?" Harrison asked.

"Because the rest of you are busy with your families. As it should be." Zach tilted his whiskey, finished the glass, and placed it back on the table.

Since they were in the city, he looked over at Raven, the manager, who liked to be hands on at The Back Door, and he gestured for another.

She inclined her head and walked back around the bar to get him his drink.

Zach turned back to his siblings in time to see Asher studying him. Intently. "What?" he asked his oldest brother.

"You let her leave?"

He raised an eyebrow at that. "Isn't that what you wanted? For Hadley to go back where she came from?"

Their other brothers grew silent.

"No, it's what I worried she'd do. What I want is for you to be happy. I didn't expect you to just let her leave." Asher raised his glass and took a sip.

"As opposed to what? Tying her to the bed to keep her here?"

Harrison chuckled.

"It'd be a start," Asher muttered.

"Only you, big brother," Nick said with a shake of his head just as Raven strode up to them.

"Refills for the table." She served everyone their drinks. "Anyone interested in food?"

Zach shook his head. "I can't get drunk if I eat. But thanks."

Everyone else declined as well.

Nick braced one arm on the table. "Asher may be all about extreme solutions but in this case, I agree with him. She's gone for ten years, you get a second chance, and you just waved goodbye?" He shook his head. "Didn't you learn anything from me? Lock that shit down!"

"Do I need to drink at my own table?"

"No, you need to go get your woman. And on that note…" Harrison rose to his feet. "I need to get home to mine. My girls are waiting for me."

"Give the kids a kiss from their favorite uncle," Zach said.

An answering groan came from around the table, making him laugh.

Nick gave a half salute and strode out to head home to his family.

Zach took another sip of his drink. He knew his siblings had a point but how could he have made Hadley stay in light of her valid arguments in favor of needing to go?

"I'm out," Asher said, rising to his feet.

"Me too." Harrison followed.

Zach gave them a forced grin. Being ditched wasn't fun. He was the last Dare standing and it sucked considering he had a woman he loved who'd opted to leave.

"Bye and give my love to the ladies and babies." That he meant with all his heart. He adored his family.

Harrison slapped him on the shoulder. Asher did too.

Once they were gone, Remy slid into an empty seat. After leaning back, he ran a hand through his brown hair.

"Where'd you come from?" Zach asked.

"I've been here. Just didn't want to interrupt your boys night."

He shook his head. "You're always welcome."

Remy lifted a shoulder in a shrug. "I have enough siblings of my own. I get needing brother time."

Remy also had three brothers and a sister, not to mention a tragic family story. But like the Dares, the Sterlings were close.

"Hi, Boss One and Boss Two." Raven strode over. She was dressed in black jeans and a tank top with The Back Door logo on the front. Her light brown hair had been pulled into a bun and she wore heavy makeup for her shift. "Another drink or food for either of you?"

Before Zach could ask for another drink, this despite the fact that he was beginning to feel the buzz, Remy rose to his feet.

"And who would I be?" he asked her.

She smirked. "Boss Two, of course. Zach's the Big Boss."

Remy rolled his eyes. "We're equal partners," he reminded her.

"Aww, do you have an inferiority complex?" she asked, patting him on the shoulder. "I'll have to think of another name for you."

He rolled his eyes. "I'd rather you didn't."

Zach chuckled. They both knew whatever she came up with would only make him feel worse. On purpose. Those two had a love-hate relationship that everyone around them felt. In other words, the sexual tension was high.

"Still no food for me." He debated another drink and decided against it. Nothing would make him feel better.

"I'm good. Thanks, Raven." Remy winked and re-took his seat.

Zach shook his head. "She's going to sue you for sexual harassment one day." He wasn't really worried. The heat was mutual.

Remy shrugged. "One day she'll realize she likes me. But let's talk about you. It's been a week since Hadley left and you're miserable."

"I already heard it from my brothers."

"Then do something about it!" He leaned back in his seat, but Zach felt his friend's frustration. "Hadley has had to handle everything herself for most of her life. She's all but Dani's mother. She thinks she needs to be independent because it's all she knows. I sense she's afraid not to be independent because she keeps losing people."

Zach ran his hand through his hair, his own irritation showing through. "I tried to show her she could lean on me," he muttered.

Remy smacked him on the side of his head. "And from what you told me, instead of pushing her hard to stay, you easily let her go. If you ask me, she needs you to do just the opposite. Fight for her. Unless you changed your mind about her?"

"Fuck no! I thought I was doing the right thing, giving her what she said she needed." Had he been wrong? "So much time had passed, I was getting to know her again. I screwed up."

Remy nodded. "But you can still make it right."

Rising to his feet, Zach glanced at his best friend and partner. "How come you can figure out my love life but not your own?"

Remy let out a low chuckle, but it wasn't one of amusement. "Did you ever try getting past Raven's walls?"

Grabbing Remy's shoulder, Zach met his gaze. "Persistence pays off and I know you. You're nothing if not persistent."

"Good luck," Remy said.

"Back at you." Now that Zach knew what to do, he needed to figure out how to accomplish his goal. He didn't want to spend another night without Hadley and Dani with him, where they belonged.

Chapter Nineteen

HADLEY DISCONNECTED THE call with the realtor who was gearing up to put a For Sale sign on the lawn soon. By the grace of God, her father owned the house free and clear. No mortgage. He hadn't put it up as collateral for any of his dirty dealings and he'd signed the deed over to Hadley. Not in person. He still refused visitation and she wouldn't ask again.

He'd also relinquished permanent custody of Dani. A judge needed to approve her status but Zach's lawyer, was in constant contact, had assured her that with both Dani's parents in prison, Hadley, as Dani's blood relative and pseudo-parent for most of her life, would be granted permanent guardianship.

As for the house, Hadley ended up hiring a junk hauling service to get rid of the broken furniture and other damaged items. Most of their possessions had been destroyed but she couldn't bring herself to care about *things*. Not when a short week ago, she thought she might lose her sister.

Dani's anger at her parents needed to be dealt with, as did the kidnapping after effects. She was healthy, mostly happy, and had agreed to talk to a therapist once they were settled in New York.

New York.

The Hamptons.

Zach.

She hadn't told him her plans. For whatever reason, she felt she needed to put this part of her life behind her before she returned and offered him her heart.

Her thoughts returned to the here and now. Without beds to sleep in, she and Dani had continued to stay in the hotel, which let Dani be in the same room with Hadley at night. As her sister insisted on sleeping with the bathroom light on and the door wide open, letting her view the entire room, Hadley felt certain she was doing right by keeping her sister close. And she did her best not to worry about the accumulating credit card bill or other costs associated with the house.

Next week, a cleaning service would come in to make the inside presentable for walk-throughs. Hadley would take whatever price she could get for the dilapidated home to pay off expenses and then she would put the remainder of the money aside for Dani's college education.

But she wasn't waiting for the house to sell. She and Dani had a flight booked to New York this evening.

"Dani?" Walking out of the kitchen, Hadley called out for her sister.

"Yeah, Hads. I'm packing up in my room," Dani yelled back.

Despite what Dani said, she'd been in touch with her friends to catch up and say goodbye. Yet she was totally on board with moving.

One thing Hadley had learned was that it was okay to lean on Zach. She planned to show up on his doorstep, surprise him, and hope they could pick up where they'd left off. She was finished pushing him away.

She wanted to move in with him and start their lives.

"Hads! Look outside!" Dani yelled again from her bedroom.

Hadley walked to the front door and pulled it open. She stepped onto the porch to see an unfamiliar car parked out front and Zach striding up the path, a determined look on his face.

She didn't stop to think what he was doing here. She didn't care. He'd merely moved up her timeline. She threw off her lingering fears and ran, meeting him halfway up the walk and jumping into his arms.

He caught her and hugged her to him, spinning her around before letting her down. He held her until her feet stabilized, and she met his gaze.

"What are you doing here?" she asked at the same time he spoke.

"You and Dani are coming home with me."

Unable to withhold her happy smile, she nodded. "We're already on tonight's flight."

Surprise flickered across his handsome face. Next thing she knew, his lips were on hers and he kissed her senseless, not ending their connection. She was so glad because she'd missed him so much. He'd come for her and now he knew she was returning to him, too.

"Hey you two, get a room!" Dani's voice sounded from her upstairs window, causing them to break apart, laughing. "You have neighbors watching." She giggled and slammed the window closed.

Zach chuckled. "She's been texting me."

"She has?"

"Who else was going to make sure my room was ready for me?" Dani had obviously come from the house in time to hear their conversation.

Hadley looked at her sister and groaned, but she couldn't withhold her continued smile. "Brat."

Zach tapped Hadley's shoulder and she met his gaze. "I had already booked my flight before Dani told me you were coming back. Asher's jet was being used for business."

"Oh, poor baby had to fly commercial," Hadley

said, lifting her hand to cup his cheek. "You came for me." She spoke in a much more serious tone.

"If I'd been thinking clearly, I'd have been here sooner, but I thought I needed to give you the space you asked for to figure things out."

She sighed. "I knew that first night I made a mistake."

"I told her so." Dani sounded proud.

Zach held out an arm and brought her sister into their small circle. "As long as we're all on the same page now. I'm bringing my girls home."

Dani sniffed, catching Hadley by surprise. "I love you, Zach."

"I love you too, kid. Now go get your bags. We're getting out of here."

Without back talk, Dani ran back to the house, leaving Hadley and Zach alone.

ZACH DIDN'T KNOW what he'd expected when he drove up to the house where Hadley had lived from the age of sixteen on, but this beat up place wasn't it. The only sign of Hadley's presence were now wilting flowers that had been planted along the front of the old shrubbery. Not that they'd lived in luxury back in New York but obviously her father had fallen onto even harder times and hadn't kept up the property.

"You're sure about this?" he asked, kicking himself for allowing her to have second thoughts. But he needed to know.

She nodded. "The house is going on the market. The realtor can deal with it through the lock box she put up." She looked around and sighed. "There's nothing for me here. My life and the people I care about are in New York. *You're* in New York."

"Your job?"

She lifted her shoulders in an unconcerned shrug. "I can tutor until I decide if I want to get my certification in New York. I'll figure things out."

"And the loan forgiveness you mentioned?"

"We'll figure that out, too."

He smiled at her answer. "We?"

She nodded. "We. I'm not going to do it all by myself. I'm open to help because I trust you to be there for me."

That was all he'd ever needed to hear. "I love you, Hads."

"I love you too, Zach."

His lips met hers and all was right in his world again.

Epilogue

Remy Sterling
One year Later – Zach and Hadley's Wedding

THE CEREMONY FOR Zach and Hadley's wedding took place in one of the ballrooms of The Meridian NYC Hotel owned by the Dare family. Remy couldn't be happier for his friend as he married the love of his life.

Serenity had walked down the aisle, a vision in silver, her jet-black hair falling to her shoulders. Zach followed, then Remy, as the best man so Zach didn't have to choose among his brothers. The bridesmaids, made up of Zach's sisters and sisters-in-law, wore pale blue and walked side by side with the groomsmen.

Layla was escorted by one of her triplet brothers, the other two following behind each other. It was, Remy thought, the biggest bridal party he'd ever seen.

Next came Hadley's sister, Dani, the maid of honor, beaming at her role in the ceremony. She'd grown up a lot in the year since she'd shown up at their restaurant with Hadley, upending Zach's life for the better.

The flower girls consisted of Zach's nieces, some

helped by their mothers, Leah, Nick's daughter, leading them all.

Remy stood beside Zach as they waited for the bride's turn to walk down the aisle. His siblings stood in a line beside them.

"Nervous?" Remy asked quietly.

Zach stretched his head from side to side. "Not a bit. Though I wouldn't mind getting rid of the monkey suit."

Shaking his head, Remy chuckled. "Once Serenity got a hold of the wedding plans, you had no choice."

"Yeah. But since she's all but adopted Hadley and Dani into the family, she can do anything she wants, and I'll go along."

Remy grinned. "You're lucky to have her." A pang hit him because he no longer had his mother in his life.

She'd been murdered sixteen years ago by one of his stockbroker father's clients. There were some details of that night Remy blamed himself for, but as usual, he pushed it out of his mind. His father, grand-parents and siblings made up a tight-knit group and Remy understood how Zach felt about his big family.

"So, how's it feel to get everything you always wanted?" Remy asked.

Zach's grin said it all. "Second chances rock."

"I'll drink to that later," Nick said from his place in

line.

The other brothers agreed with Nick.

"Are you going to make your move on Raven tonight?" Zach asked him, his gaze going back to the closed doors Hadley stood behind.

Raven. The Back Door NYC bar manager and the woman who'd captured Remy's interest from the moment he'd met her. Their flirting was fun, but he was aware she had walls built to keep people out. Over time, he'd become more invested in finding out why and being the man to break through her reserve.

"I'll do my best," he said, knowing he intended to have a slow dance with her so he could feel her lithe body against his.

Zach opened his mouth to speak when "Here Comes the Bride" started. The men clasped their hands in front of them and waited as the doors at the far end of the aisle opened.

Hadley stood beside Zach's father, who was walking her down the aisle. Zach didn't take his eyes off his soon-to-be-wife.

The ceremony was short and beautiful and soon Zach had Hadley in his arms, his lips on hers, the wedding guests cheering.

Remy's gaze strayed to Raven, who wore a beautiful green dress, her tanned skin glowing as she sat in the audience, her eyes tear-filled, like many of the female guests. None as beautiful as she was.

All the Dare siblings had found their person, leaving Remy the single man left in the group. With his gaze pinned on the woman of *his* dreams, Remy was determined... his turn was next.

Thanks for reading! What's next?

Remy Sterling and the Sterling Family ... with visits by the Kingstons and Dares.

Read JUST ONE MORE MOMENT!

JUST ONE MORE MOMENT

A billionaire, workplace, friends to lovers romance with a possessive, hot, protective alpha hero.

Billionaire Remington Sterling has had his eye on gorgeous waitress Raven Walsh ever since she started working at The Back Door bar in New York City. Now that he is a co-owner and on premises, he is determined to convince Raven he's worth the risk.

But Raven has a secret past, one she is not only running from but is petrified will catch up to her. When it does, in the form of an obsessive stepbrother, she must decide if Remy is the right man to trust or whether it's time to run.

Good thing Remy is one step ahead of her...

Read JUST ONE MORE MOMENT

Want even more Carly books?

CARLY'S BOOKLIST by Series – visit:
https://www.carlyphillips.com/CPBooklist

Sign up for Carly's Newsletter:
https://www.carlyphillips.com/CPNewsletter

Join Carly's Corner on Facebook:
https://www.carlyphillips.com/CarlysCorner

Carly on Facebook:
https://www.carlyphillips.com/CPFanpage

Carly on Instagram:
https://www.carlyphillips.com/CPInstagram

Carly's Booklist

The Dare Series

Dare to Love Series
Book 1: Dare to Love (Ian & Riley)
Book 2: Dare to Desire (Alex & Madison)
Book 3: Dare to Touch (Dylan & Olivia)
Book 4: Dare to Hold (Scott & Meg)
Book 5: Dare to Rock (Avery & Grey)
Book 6: Dare to Take (Tyler & Ella)
A Very Dare Christmas – Short Story (Ian & Riley)

** Sienna Dare gets together with Ethan Knight in **The Knight Brothers** (Dare Me Tonight).*

** Jason Dare gets together with Faith in the **Sexy Series** (More Than Sexy).*

Dare NY Series (NY Dare Cousins)
Book 1: Dare to Surrender (Gabe & Isabelle)
Book 2: Dare to Submit (Decklan & Amanda)
Book 3: Dare to Seduce (Max & Lucy)

The Knight Brothers
Book 1: Take Me Again (Sebastian & Ashley)
Book 2: Take Me Down (Parker & Emily)
Book 3: Dare Me Tonight (Ethan Knight & Sienna Dare)
Novella: Take The Bride (Sierra & Ryder)
Take Me Now – Short Story (Harper & Matt)

The Sexy Series

Book 1: More Than Sexy (Jason Dare & Faith)

Book 2: Twice As Sexy (Tanner & Scarlett)

Book 3: Better Than Sexy (Landon & Vivienne)

Novella: Sexy Love (Shane & Amber)

Dare Nation

Book 1: Dare to Resist (Austin & Quinn)

Book 2: Dare to Tempt (Damon & Evie)

Book 3: Dare to Play (Jaxon & Macy)

Book 4: Dare to Stay (Brandon & Willow)

Novella: Dare to Tease (Hudson & Brianne)

* Paul Dare's sperm donor kids

Kingston Family

Book 1: Just One Night (Linc Kingston & Jordan Greene)

Book 2: Just One Scandal (Chloe Kingston & Beck Daniels)

Book 3: Just One Chance (Xander Kingston & Sasha Keaton)

Book 4: Just One Spark (Dash Kingston & Cassidy Forrester)

Just One Wish (Axel Forrester)

Book 5: Just One Dare (Aurora Kingston & Nick Dare)

Book 6: Just One Kiss

Book 7: Just One Taste
Book 8: Just Another Spark
Book 9: Just One Fling
Book 10: Just One Tease
Book 11: Just One More Moment

For the most recent Carly books, visit CARLY'S BOOKLIST page
www.carlyphillips.com/CPBooklist

Other Indie Series

Billionaire Bad Boys
Book 1: Going Down Easy
Book 2: Going Down Hard
Book 3: Going Down Fast
Book 4: Going In Deep
Going Down Again – Short Story

Hot Heroes Series
Book 1: Touch You Now
Book 2: Hold You Now
Book 3: Need You Now
Book 4: Want You Now

Bodyguard Bad Boys
Book 1: Rock Me
Book 2: Tempt Me
Novella: His To Protect

For the most recent Carly books, visit CARLY'S BOOKLIST page
www.carlyphillips.com/CPBooklist

Carly's Originally Traditionally Published Books

Serendipity Series
Book 1: Serendipity
Book 2: Kismet
Book 3: Destiny
Book 4: Fated
Book 5: Karma

Serendipity's Finest Series
Book 1: Perfect Fit
Book 2: Perfect Fling
Book 3: Perfect Together
Book 4: Perfect Strangers

The Chandler Brothers
Book 1: The Bachelor
Book 2: The Playboy
Book 3: The Heartbreaker

Hot Zone
Book 1: Hot Stuff
Book 2: Hot Number
Book 3: Hot Item
Book 4: Hot Property

Costas Sisters
Book 1: Under the Boardwalk
Book 2: Summer of Love

Lucky Series
Book 1: Lucky Charm
Book 2: Lucky Break
Book 3: Lucky Streak

Bachelor Blogs
Book 1: Kiss Me if You Can
Book 2: Love Me If You Dare

Ty and Hunter
Book 1: Cross My Heart
Book 2: Sealed with a Kiss

Carly Classics (Unexpected Love)
Book 1: The Right Choice
Book 2: Perfect Partners
Book 3: Unexpected Chances
Book 4: Worthy of Love

Carly Classics (The Simply Series)
Book 1: Simply Sinful
Book 2: Simply Scandalous
Book 3: Simply Sensual
Book 4: Body Heat
Book 5: Simply Sexy

For the most recent Carly books, visit CARLY'S BOOKLIST page

www.carlyphillips.com/CPBooklist

Carly's Still Traditionally Published Books

Stand-Alone Books

Brazen

Secret Fantasy

Seduce Me

The Seduction

More Than Words Volume 7 – Compassion Can't Wait

Naughty Under the Mistletoe

Grey's Anatomy 101 Essay

For the most recent Carly books, visit CARLY'S BOOKLIST page

www.carlyphillips.com/CPBooklist

About the Author

NY Times, Wall Street Journal, and USA Today Bestseller, Carly Phillips is the queen of Alpha Heroes, at least according to The Harlequin Junkie Reviewer. Carly married her college sweetheart and lives in Purchase, NY along with her crazy dogs who are featured on her Facebook and Instagram pages. The author of over 75 romance novels, she has raised two incredible daughters and is now an empty nester. Carly's book, The Bachelor, was chosen by Kelly Ripa as her first romance club pick. Carly loves social media and interacting with her readers. Want to keep up with Carly? Sign up for her newsletter and receive TWO FREE books at www.carlyphillips.com.

Made in United States
North Haven, CT
04 November 2023

43607789R00153